Anonymous

Ada Moore's Story

Vol. II

Anonymous

Ada Moore's Story
Vol. II

ISBN/EAN: 9783337040598

Printed in Europe, USA, Canada, Australia, Japan

Cover: Foto ©Andreas Hilbeck / pixelio.de

More available books at **www.hansebooks.com**

ADA MOORE'S STORY.

A NOVEL.

IN THREE VOLUMES.

VOL. II.

LONDON:
TINSLEY BROTHERS, 18 CATHERINE STREET,
STRAND.
1867.

ADA MOORE'S STORY.

CHAPTER I.

SIR JAMES MOORE, K.C.B.

THE arrival of my uncle in London accelerated the departure of the Hodgson family. Although I had not much sympathy with their tastes, feelings, or pursuits, yet as they had always been kind to me and I had known them all my life, I wept to think that I should probably never see them again at Moordell Hall.

Mrs. Hodgson looked ill, anxious, and wretched, but she said nothing more on the subject of her troubles to my mother. It was quite clear she had not had courage to follow my mother's good advice, and she was ashamed to own her moral cowardice. Poor old Hodgson, deceived by his wife and son, had taken Smithkin into partnership.

As soon as the Hodgsons were gone, workmen filled the Hall. Builders too were busy there. As my uncle had not requested my father to superintend their movements, or to look over the place, or in any way to interest himself in what was going on, he, hurt and even perhaps a little offended, neither visited Moordell himself nor encouraged us to do so.

We heard, however, of great works going on there,—of an addition to the house, built on to it in the Indian style, from a plan sent down by Sir James himself,—of what Bessie called "all manner o' ootlondish contrivances,"—and of vans of furniture of the costliest description, and much of it Indian.

We heard that my uncle was in town, long before he wrote to us to announce his arrival there. When he did so, my father, whose warm heart yearned towards this cold, eccentric brother, resolved to go up to London to welcome him back to his native land. He did not stay very long, and he seemed rather disappointed in his brother's reception.

In his letter to my mother he said, "Twenty-five years in India have altered James so that when first I saw him I did not recognize him at all. I fear he is out of health: the liver is affected most likely, for he is very yellow; even the whites of his eyes have a deep yellow tinge. He is reserved, cold, and very sarcastic, and seems so little disposed to be brotherly that I shall get back to my dear warm home and my affectionate darlings, as soon as I can."

My father came home to us on Tuesday; and on the following Sunday, to my great surprise, I saw a bald old guinea-coloured little man, with keen black eyes and a very shrivelled skin, in the squire's pew. I felt certain that it *was* Sir James, and I was much disappointed, for I had always fancied that my father's brother must bear at least a family likeness to my father.

Alas! I never saw two people more entirely unlike in every respect,—form, feature, colouring, but expression above all. My father's noble face beamed with intellect and love; my uncle's had a kind of worldly shrewdness, but the prevading expression was one of suspicion and sarcasm. I feared him from the first moment I met his cold, keen eyes; I tried not to hate him.

We had had no notice of his arrival, which must have taken place in the night. He hurried out of church and back to the Hall, so that to speak to him was impossible. He did the same at afternoon church. As my

father and mother never paid any visits on
Sunday, they resolved to call upon him the
next day. I accompanied them. A black
footman said massa was gone to Alnwick;
and I own I felt it a relief not to see him.

On the third day from that of our call, he
returned the visit.

"How glad you must be to find yourself
in old England once more, Sir James!" said
my mother.

"Why no, Ma'am," he replied. "I in-
finitely prefer India. I like to see the sun,
and feel it too ; I have not been warm since
I've been in this land of east winds, fogs,
and taxes."

"But the dear old Hall—you are glad to
be there at last ? The Hall—"

"Looks much smaller than I had pictured
it to myself," he replied. "I believe our
memories always exaggerate the size and
beauty of the places we loved in boyhood. And

so," he added, turning to me, "that young lady is the last female scion of our race. You should have sent her out to me : I'd have got her a husband at Bombay : girls, if they play their cards well, are sure to marry there !"

"But what cards has Adie to play?" said my mother, smiling.

"Youth, good looks, good blood," he said, "and, I hope I may add, that queen of trumps, a sensible mother."

Even he, crabbed as he was, seemed to sun himself in my mother's smile, and to thaw as he spoke to her.

My father came in from visiting some of the poor in a distant part of his parish, while my uncle was still there. He begged Sir James to stay to dinner.

Sir James replied—

"No, I thank you. I never dine out, and I never give dinners. I live quite by rule;

and, as I have an invalid friend staying with me who has made it a stipulation that no strangers shall be admitted, I cannot at present ask you and your women-folk to the Hall; but I want to have a long talk with you some day soon, and I will therefore call again shortly."

My father was naturally mortified by this strange and unnatural conduct. Soon, however, rumour became rife in the parish which seemed to throw some light upon the mystery. It was said that in that strange " outlandish wing" which Sir James had caused to be added to the Hall, an Indian lady and her female attendants lived.

Some workmen engaged about the building, which was not quite completed, deposed to having seen, through a skylight they were inserting, a dark-skinned, rather stout lady, with Eastern features and with a turban on her head, wrapt up in rich shawls

and glittering with jewels, lying on a sort
of ottoman propped up by cushions, while
black slaves fanned her, and offered her refreshments on gold salvers. A young fellow,
also very dark, who was supposed to be some
page in attendance on Sir James, was often
seen in the park, and sometimes riding about
the country.

Of course, all sorts of stories were afloat.
My father, however, remembered that many
years back—during some of the never-ending
rebellions and disturbances in India—his
brother, even then high in command, had
been mentioned in the papers as having
sheltered and protected a Begum and some
of her attendants. He thought it very likely
this gorgeous lady might be that very Eastern
princess. He refuted and resented, with
much displeasure, all slanderous reports and
evil constructions put by busy calumny on
the presence of the dark lady and her suite
at Moordell Hall.

However, it in a manner accounted for my uncle's not inviting us to go there. Of course, with such a mysterious visitor under Sir James's roof, my mother had no wish to be received herself there, nor to take me there.

I am sure my father was much disappointed. I think he had looked forward to being a good deal at his old ancestral Hall. He had anticipated the pleasure of fishing in the Coquet by his brother's side, as they had done in boyhood,—of sitting under the fine old trees which had shaded so many generations of Moores of Moordell,—in fact, of feeling himself once more at home in the old gallery of family portraits, and among the Lares and Penates of his ancestors. No wonder, if so, he was disappointed. As it was, Moordell Hall was much less accessible to us than it had been in the time of the Hodgsons.

One day my father was gone to visit the wife of Sir James's gamekeeper. She was dangerously ill, and had sent for "his reverence." My father set out immediately, begging me to come to him with a basket containing wine and other restoratives for the sick woman.

There was a short cut to the gamekeeper's cottage, across the northern extremity of the park. A gate and a stile divided it from a patch of furze—grouse common, or moorland, in which the gamekeeper's cottage stood. Since Sir James's return several large boards, painted white, had been placed at different entrances to the park. On these boards the words — "No Thoroughfare. Trespassers will be Prosecuted. Beware of Spring-guns and Man-traps"—were painted in black. One of these boards was fixed to a tree close to the stile and gate in question. As I hurried along with my basket on

my arm, I heard footsteps behind me. I
had no doubt they were those of the gamekeeper's son, or some kind neighbour going
to see the poor man's sick wife.

I turned round, expecting to see a familiar
face. But no; a strange-looking, very thin
and lithe form met my view. It was that
of a youth, apparently about eighteen, with
Hindoo features, dark olive skin, long, glittering, jet-black eyes and hair, and a white
turban wound round his head. His costume
was Eastern; and as he passed me he grinned
from ear to ear, showing two rows of pearly
teeth in a mouth of very bright scarlet.
His manner was so wild and odd, that I felt
certain he was what the Borderers call
"daft," and I was glad to see him hurrying
on before me.

Close to the stile and the gate were two
clumps of very dark firs; on one side they
joined the plantation, which formed the

northern extremity of the park ; on the other they stood alone, on a wild patch of moorland.

I had little doubt that the youth who had just passed me, grinning in my face and saying some mocking words in Hindostanee, was the same who was said to be located at Moordell Hall, and to be so high in favour with my uncle that he often walked and even rode out with him, and dined at the same table with him.

He had the reputation of being a very idle, mischievous young fellow, agile as a monkey, and fond of talking to himself.

Some people said he was the son of the " dark lady," the Eastern princess, as he had access to her apartments,—a liberty which a Hindoo lady of high caste would not have granted to any but her husband or her son.

Many stories were told of the spiteful

tricks and mischievous pranks played by this youth, and I was very glad to think he was out of sight, when, just as I reached the gate, from among the fir-trees and the fern in which he had been lying in ambush, he sprang on to the gate, and, sitting astride upon it like the village boy in the clever picture " Happy as a King," grinned, shouted, and, laughing aloud, pointed to the white board, and said in a foreign accent, " No Thoroughfare." He then said something in Hindostanee, which I could not understand, but which, from his absurd pantomime, I understood to mean that he would not let me pass without a kiss.

Inexpressibly annoyed, I left the gate, and was about to get over the stile, when, with a bound worthy of an acrobat, he perched himself upon it. Again I moved to the gate, and again he was there !

I then resolved to go back to the Vicarage,

to send Bessie with the basket to the gamekeeper's cottage; but, as if resolved to prevent my escape, he sprang from the gate,
and began dancing round me.

I did not know what to do, and tears of
annoyance were in my eyes. At this moment, to my inexpressible relief, I saw my
father drawing near. Another moment and
he was at the gate. The tormentor, who
had his back to the gate, did not see him.

My father comprehended at a glance the
dilemma in which I was. All the old
Border blood in his veins boiled when he
saw this mountebank, as he called him, trying to embrace his daughter.

In the passion of the moment he seized
the dark youth by the scarf that formed his
sash, and having a horsewhip in his hand—
for he had been just about to mount his
horse when he was sent for—he administered
a severe thrashing to the astounded youth,

who writhed, wriggled, shrieked, roared, and whined.

Vainly I implored my father to desist. Never had I seen him in a passion before; but I had heard him say that in his early youth he had been subject at times to fits of rage, which he had succeeded in mastering by reflection and resolution.

At length, having in some degree exhausted his passion, he flung the youth from him, and, the dark Hindoo face coming in contact with the rough bark of a fir-tree, the blood oozed from his cheek.

"A mere scratch," said my father, seeing me turn pale. "He is not hurt," he added, as the youth rose and ran with the speed of a hunted hare across the park in the direction of the Hall.

"It is these treacherous Hindoo inmates," said my father bitterly, "that prevent my having access to the home of my childhood and the heart of my brother. We will take those things to the cottage, Ada, and then I will see you safe home, for I want to ride over to Morpeth at once."

CHAPTER II.

THE next day, before we had quite done breakfast, Sir James was announced by Bessie. He was deadly pale, and there was a very angry light in his eyes, and a forced smile on his face.

"I am come to talk to you on business," he said to my father; "but first I wish to know by what right you presume to inflict personal chastisement on a youth under my protection?"

"If you mean that young Indian mounte-

C

bank, James," said my father, "he insulted my daughter, and—

"Mountebank, Sir!" said my uncle, livid with rage. "That youth has royal blood in his veins!"

"If he were a king and he insulted my daughter, I would thrash him as I would a dog, and as I did that half-witted lad."

"Half-witted!" hissed my uncle between his closed teeth.

"No, perhaps not *quite* half-witted," said my father. "I do not think he *is* quite half-witted."

My uncle bit his lip and clenched his hands, but presently said, "You horse-whipped that noble boy, and you even shed his blood, because he would not allow you and your daughter to trespass."

"To *trespass!* Ada and I to *trespass* at Moordell. You are joking, brother. How could we trespass where I was born, and where *you* are master? Brother," he added, the tears standing in his eyes, "we two brothers are the last of a time-honoured race. Do not let strangers from north or south, east or west, come between us. Do not talk of *my* trespassing on *your* estate! I am sorry if I have hurt any one you are interested in, but I contend no father could have done less. I did not even know who the boy was. Do not let a stranger come between us, and do not talk of my trespassing, or of my child's trespassing, where, as boys, we used to roam and play together, and plan all we should do when your dreams should be realized, and you should come back from foreign parts to keep the old place up in the old style as Moore of Moordell."

He held out his hand to my uncle, who took it and seemed a little moved. And thus peace was restored.

Presently Sir James said, "Is your life insured?"

"No," said my father. "I have often thought of insuring it, but that fond silly wife of mine never would agree to it."

"I could not bear the thought of his stinting himself in life, in order to leave money to me at his death. What use would it be to me then? I could not survive him."

"Romantic folly!" said my uncle; "and quite unworthy of a sensible woman and a good mother! You could and would survive him; and you would find a few thousands a great balm to your sorrow, Ma'am. Every married man ought to insure his life!"

"But he cannot afford it."

"Then I will afford it for him," said my uncle. "What say you? Do you agree? I will keep up the policy for you."

"I shall be very glad and very grateful,"

said my father; "and so will you be, my
love," he added, addressing my mother, who
had walked to the window in order that Sir
James might not see, and jeer at, the tears
in her eyes. "I shall die none the sooner
—nay, I shall perhaps live all the longer,
for the comfort it will be to me to think—"

"Oh, say no more about it!" cried my
mother, fairly bursting into tears. "Do as
you will, but never speak on the dreadful
subject again!"

"Very well!" said Sir James sarcasti-
cally. "As you have given him *carte
blanche*, Mrs. Moore, I shall take him to
town with me by the 6.15 A.M. train to-
morrow. I hope it won't be quite so affecting to you to hear me speak of my death;
but, as I understand that Miss Ada, there,
has engaged herself to a poor man, when
Fenwick of Fenwick would have gladly
taken her to wife, I was going to kill two

birds with one stone. I mean to make a new will, and insure my brother's life. So now I will take my leave. Good-bye, Mrs. Moore; good-bye, Miss Ada."

"I will walk with you to the park gates, James," said my father.

"What a very strange person your uncle is, Ada!" said my mother. "I hate this plan for insuring your father's life. I hope Sir James has no idea of marrying."

＊   ＊   ＊   ＊

My father soon returned.

"I cannot make my brother out," he said. "He talks of leaving Ada twenty thousand pounds."

"Yes," said my mother; "he knows his life is not a good one; and, as you would inherit the estate, he, now he knows Ada is engaged, and to a man of no fortune, means to leave her twenty thousand pounds. And very kind too!"

" But why, if so, does he want me to insure my life ? "

" Oh, that is some whim. I hate to think of it," said my mother ; " but I suppose we must humour him ! "

" I'm delighted to do it, as James will keep up the policy, and bear all the expenses," said my father. " I suppose the young mountebank I horsewhipped is a native prince—son of the Begum James protected and sheltered. Well, prince or peasant, I've given him a lesson he won't forget in a hurry ! "

That evening my dear father was in very high spirits. The late post brought me a letter from Roscommon. My father asked me to read him some parts of it, and he praised the style, and said—

" I dare say I shall grow to like him in time, Ada ; but, Mamma, he comes to rob us of our darling, and parents are apt to be selfish ! "

My dear father! I never saw him so
merry as he was on that evening. He told
us lively stories of his college days. He
sang duets with my mother, and formed all
sorts of plans for the future. He insisted
on our partaking of some grog he mixed for
himself, and made old Bessie drink 'health
and long life' to him and to us, in a glass of
his 'brew,' as he called it. He wanted not
to go to bed, as he had to be up so early,
but my mother would not hear of such an
arrangement. So we all retired at midnight,
and at five we met again in the breakfast-
room.

He was still in very high spirits, but my
mother was pale and rather depressed.

He asked me for Roscommon Lyall's address, and said he should probably call on
him, and bring him down, if he could, to
spend a week or two at the Vicarage; for
that he felt he had been ungracious and un-

kind to his dear girl's choice, his future son-in-law!

At this moment Bessie came in to say that the pony-chaise was at the door.

It was a lovely autumn morning, and my mother suddenly proposed to go with him to the station to see him off, adding that she could drive herself back. My father gladly assented, and embraced me fervently. He smiled when he found that I had not only written Roscommon's address, but a note to my beloved for him to deliver!

He was still laughing at this little incident as I stood at the Vicarage gate, with Bessie, watching till the pony-chaise had turned the corner. They were out of sight when Bessie said—

"Look, Miss, what a flight o' crows! I hate the sight of 'em, they're na canny."

CHAPTER III.

THE DREAD PRESENCE.

I HAVE now reached a point in my early history which it requires all my fortitude to enable me to record. Many years have passed since that dreadful day, but yet my hand trembles, my heart beats, and hot tears blind-me, as I recall it. I cannot expatiate on it; I can only state the dreadful facts.

My mother had been all day much depressed in spirit. She said that the idea of my father insuring his life for our benefit had brought vividly before her the possibility of her surviving him. She added that, though she was some years his junior, yet that he had always been so strong and well, and she herself so delicate and weakly, that she had always taken it for granted she should go first. Now the possibility of her being one day that desolate creature, a widow, haunted her, and she could not shake it off.

I did my best to argue that darling mother and devoted wife out of these strange and gloomy presentiments. I persuaded her to take a little walk with me. The air roused her, and she seemed to rally a little.

*　　*　　*　　*　　*

I was presiding at our tea-table when our dear old family doctor rang at the bell. I saw him at the gate. I opened the glass door of the sitting-room that looked on the lawn, and hurried out myself to admit him and bring him in to tea.

I thought his lively genial converse, full of anecdote and humour, would enliven my mother. But when I saw his face, I felt certain something dreadful had happened. Generally smiling and rubicund, he was now ghastly pale. He trembled and could hardly articulate.

"What is it, Doctor?" I cried. "For Heaven's sake speak! What is it?"

Near the gate was an arbour. He led the way to it and entered it. There was a bench and a rustic table. He sank on the seat, crossed his arms on the table, buried his face in his hands, and wept,— nay, sobbed.

My mother, surprised that we did not enter the house, came out in search of us. Not seeing us at the gate or on the lawn, she glanced anxiously round, and perceived my white dress gleaming through the leaves and trellis-work.

Hearing her voice calling "Ada, Ada," Dr. Tweedale looked up and said, "I cannot tell *her*,—no, I cannot tell *her ;* it will kill her on the spot."

"What will kill her?" I cried. "Has anything happened to my father?"

He did not answer at first, then said, "Ada, bear up for your poor mother's sake. Your father—is—no more. A railway accident—a collision between the express and a cattle train." An irrepressible shriek burst from my very heart. My mother rushed to the spot.

"Speak!" she cried, seizing Dr. Tweedale by the arm. "Speak! My husband! my love! my all!—is—dead!"

Dr. Tweedale cast down the tearful eyes into which she was gazing almost fiercely.

The next moment she sank insensible on the lawn.

"Control your own grief, Ada, my dear

child," said the doctor. " She has now no
comfort, no prop, no hope, but in you."

*   *   *   *   *

The next week of my life remains in my
memory as nothing but a chaos.

Darkened rooms, moans, groans, and
tears ; my mother alternately wild, dis-
tracted, and shrieking in her anguish, or
shaken by hysterical sobbing or more dreadful laughter, or lying insensible, and looking
as if the prayers of her despair had been
heard, and Death had reunited her to her
beloved.

Another vision of that dreadful week was
that of Bessie sitting by a fireless kitchen
grate, with her apron over her head, rocking
herself to and fro, and wailing even ; and of
the Count and the Signore, sitting in the
once cheerful, now darkened dining-room,
pale and weeping ; and at length of a
dreadful object which met my view as I

went down in the dead of the third night to
kneel by my father's old arm-chair. A coffin,—a large, long, black coffin,—my father's
coffin,—met my view. His dear and man-
gled remains were, of course, inside. I
have heard since that I was found in the
morning insensible on the floor.

Everything that passed during that dreadful week seems to me like a vision or a
dream. I know that the draper from Warkworth came and unrolled black crape, and
paramatta, and silk. I remember even the
professional jerk with which he did it, and
the tone in which he said, "The best article,
Miss, is cheapest in the end." I remember
that the dress-maker suggested, and that I
acquiesced; that the Alnwick milliner sent
black bonnets and—oh, ghastly sight, re-
opening every sluice of tears and every
bleeding wound!—widows' caps.

I heard that my uncle had shared my

father's fate, but that he had not been killed on the spot like my father. He, it seemed, had lingered a little while in great bodily agony and delirium, at the Railway Hotel at Derby, and then had died without one moment of consciousness.

I knew that my uncle's remains had been taken to the Hall, but that the two brothers were to be buried in the family vault in Moordell churchyard on the following Thursday, a week after the fatal accident.

Great was the sympathy of the whole neighbourhood, and, indeed, of all that part of the county.

The Duke and Duchess called and sent repeatedly. So did all our neighbours.

Alas, in such a grief, at least in its first wild anguish, how vain, how idle, how impertinent almost, seems all human sympathy and condolence!

On the morning of the third day, I received a few lines from Roscommon. They were dated " Paris." He said :—

" Oh, my Ada, I have this moment heard the dreadful news. I start immediately for Moordell. 1 may be of some comfort—some use. How my heart bleeds for you and your angel mother! My tears blind me. Tell her she has a son. Perhaps I shall arrive as soon as this letter,—before it, if possible. Ada! my love! my bride elect! my wife that is to be! bear up for my sake. —Your devoted, ROSCOMMON LYALL."

Two hours after the receipt of this letter, I was sitting by his side in the darkened sitting-room.

He was shocked at the ravages grief had already made in my face and form. Intense grief is not an amiable feeling; it is always tinged with remorse, founded or unfounded.

I could not listen to his words of love, nor endure the slightest caress, nor even let him hold my hand. It seemed sacrilege, while in the next room my father, who had not cordially approved of my choice, lay shrouded and coffined in his last long sleep. Roscommon *would* talk of my uncle, and to me, irritable in my agony, my uncle did not appear what he was, a fellow-victim. He seemed the cause of my father's death, of my mother's dangerous illness and despair, and of my own desolation. Roscommon was very patient and gentle with me, and I begged his forgiveness for my fretful, fitful mood, and told him I had not slept since I had heard the dreadful news, and that when I was more myself I should love him as before, and appreciate all his kindness. He told me he meant to officiate at the funeral as chief mourner. Who else had any right to do so?

He went to Mr. Laste, the undertaker, himself. He spoke as one in authority. And when Mr. Laste understood that he was engaged to me, he recognised him as the person whose orders were to be obeyed, and whose word was law !

*   *   *   *

Oh ! what a dreadful day was that of the double funeral !

Dr. Tweedale had administered a powerful sedative to my dear mother, in order that she might not hear the funeral bell. Yet even in her opiatic sleep it seemed to mix its solemn voice with her dreams ; for her moans, as it sounded like a solemn warning, were heartrending.

To me every knell seemed to strike upon my heart. I spent all that dreadful time on my knees by my bedside, weeping, praying, and holding my hands to my ears.

CHAPTER IV.

AFTER THE FUNERAL.

AFTER the funeral Roscommon sent to beg
to see me in the breakfast-room. I was surprised and annoyed to find the late darkened
house full of light. The windows were all
thrown open, and the afternoon sun came
streaming in glaring and brassy, as it seemed
to me, on my father's garden hat and great-
coat hanging in the hall, his creel, his fishing tackle, and many things so painfully as-
sociated with him, that; quite overcome, I
sank in a hall chair and wept convulsively.

At this moment Bessie, in deep mourning and looking very ill and very old, came forward, carrying a tray in her hands. She was taking sherry and sandwiches into the breakfast-room.

" Bessie," I said, " who ordered you to let this dreadful sun into this house of mourning ?"

" Mr. Lyall told me to open all the windows, Miss. Oh, he's more master here nor ever poor dear—" Here she broke down. I rose and went into the morning-room.

"Shut out the sun, Roscommon !" I said ; " I cannot bear it. It seems to mock my anguish."

He obeyed.

" My love," he said, "I have gone through it all for your sake. How is our mother, dearest? It was all done as my darling would have wished. I was chief mourner. There was a strange Indian-looking young fellow in long robes like a priest, who would walk by my side, and who sobbed convulsively all the time. Do you know who he is ?"

" Oh, I don't care who he is—what does it matter? He's an Indian prince, I believe," I said, " son of a Begum my uncle sheltered and saved in the late rebellion."

" And that young Moordell Claude Melnotte," added Roscommon with a smile, " he was there. Poor fellow! he looked dreadfully ill and cut up, and fell down insensible when— But I will not say a word more. You cannot bear it, my darling."

" Go on," I said, " I am stronger now."

" The French Count and the Signore were in agonies of grief," he added, " and all the people of any importance, far and near, followed. But the poor, their grief was very affecting. They were mourners indeed, my Ada !"

" He was so good to the poor," I sobbed.

" He was," said Roscommon with deep feeling. " He was the noblest and the best man I ever met with ; and when I think of what you have lost in him I hate myself for my jealous discontent at finding that in this deluge love has been swept from your heart, Ada ; but not for long, I hope."

" Oh, not at all !" I cried, " not for one moment. I never loved you better, O Roscommon, than I do now."

And it was true. I felt, as he sat beside me so full of sympathy and resignation, so tender and so true, that all was not lost. I had a future before me. My head began to revive. I would conquer my useless despair, my morbid remorse, and live to comfort my poor mother and to be comforted by my affianced lover.

" Roscommon," I cried, as I placed my hand in his, " love has not been swept away.

He has resumed his empire. I am yours once more."

Bessie now came in with the tray. Roscommon compelled me to take a glass of wine and a sandwich. He told me my uncle's will was to be read on the morrow at the Hall—that his lawyer had told him so at the funeral, and had invited him to be present.

Bessie reappeared at this moment, to say that my mother was awake and had asked for me; and thanking Roscommon for all his kindness, all his tenderness, and all his patience with me, and feeling, as the first poignancy of my grief abated a little, that my heart had indeed opened again to love and confidence, I allowed him to press me to his heart, and hurried to my mother's room.

Poor dear mother! she was so restless I could not leave her again, and Roscommon dined alone.

CHAPTER V.

MY UNCLE'S WILL, AND ITS RESULTS.

THE next morning my heart and mind were
in a much less morbid state, and on waking
I smiled through my tears for my father at
the thought of Roscommon's devoted love.

He had not slept at the Vicarage, but at a
little inn called the 'Moor's Head,' a very
clean, snug, and cozy place ; the landlady
having formerly been a servant in my grand-
father's family.

On this day love and grief divided my
heart. I reproached myself when I remem-

bered that under the influence of the latter I
had not shown a proper sense of Roscommon's devotion. I will make it up to him
yet, I thought; and hearing a man's firm
step first on the gravel-walk and then in the
hall, I dried my tears and hurried into the
breakfast-room.

" Oh, Roscommon!" I said, addressing
the tall form in deep mourning looking from
the window, "I *am* so glad to see you,
dearest."

At my words the figure turned round,
and I found myself face to face with Harry
Blake. He was ghastly pale. His eyes
were red and swollen with weeping. He
trembled, and could not speak. He was indeed a chief mourner.

After a while he told me that he had been
at Interlachen with some pupils of his,
under-graduates of Oxford, on an autumnal
tour, when, in ' Galignani's Messenger,' he

saw the dreadful news; that he had set out as soon as he had found some one to whom to confide his pupils: that done, that he had travelled night and day, and had arrived in time to be at my father's funeral; that he felt so very ill after that sad ceremony, he had been obliged to go back to the old house with the Count, and by his advice had gone to bed.   He came now to know if he could be of any service to my mother or to me, and to express his unutterable grief and sympathy.   He added, he must hurry back to his pupils at Interlachen, as the graduate under whose care he had left them could not prolong his stay.

Harry Blake then took his leave.

The Count and the Signore called, but as I was with my mother they would not disturb me; and at last evening closed in, dark and stormy: but no Roscommon!

One sad effect of such a grief and such a

loss as mine is, that it shakes our faith in
life and happiness.

I was in an increased terror lest some
disaster might have happened to Roscommon.

*   *   *   *

After a restless night I rose, and Bessie
brought me a letter. It was in *his* hand.
I tore it open.

The first words struck a chill to my heart,
and curdled the blood in my veins. It was
as follows :—

"My dear Friend—"

Friend! I, who had hitherto been addressed by every endearing name Love's
lexicon could furnish! Friend! This from
him!

"I cannot disguise from myself that my
attentions are no longer welcome,—that my
devotion seems to you officious, and my
affection wearisome. I am certain that but

for the extreme kindness of your heart, you would gladly break off our engagement. I, then, in justice to you, take the initiative, and give you back your freedom. But while I resign the title of your affianced lover, I hope to be allowed to retain that of your friend,

"ROSCOMMON LYALL."

For some time I sat with this cruel letter in my hand, cold, insensible, petrified.

Dr. Tweedale came in to see my mother. He found me in this state.

"My poor child," he said, "I guess it all. I foresaw it all. As soon as I heard that your uncle had left a wife and son, and that you were not only *not* the heiress of Moordell, but not even mentioned in the will, I said to myself, that fortune-hunter Lyall will break off his engagement."

"My uncle married!" I gasped out. "My uncle has left a wife and a son!"

"Yes, my child," he said. "I saw Marston, his solicitor, and he told me that for more than twenty years your uncle has been privately married to the Begum, or Indian princess, whom he saved and sheltered at Bombay. It seems she became a Christian, and had a son born in wedlock, but the whole matter was kept secret,—on her account, and by her wish. However, Sir James's conscience smote him a little about you and your father, and he told Marston he should insure your father's life, and secure you, on your coming of age or marrying, twenty thousand pounds. He was going to do this, and make several alterations in his will, when this dreadful accident cut him off. The will, unaltered as it was, was read aloud at Moordell Hall yesterday. The Begum,—or, rather, Lady Moore,—closely veiled, sat behind the curtain of the music gallery in the old hall, to hear it.

Her son, Selim, is now master of Moordell; and his mother, the Begum, is very handsomely provided for. Mr. Roscommon Lyall was present when the will was read. I heard he turned alternately white and red as he listened, and begged to be allowed to examine the document. Being convinced that it was duly witnessed, signed, and sealed, he hurried back to the Moor's Head, and dined there, after which he went up to town by the 4.30 train."

"But," said the kind old doctor, "don't fret about him, my child. Think how much better it is to have found him out before than after marriage. Come, my love, to your poor mother; she is a little better to-day, but she requires all your care."

I obeyed, and tried to rouse myself.

Alas! nothing crushes the heart like the fall of an idol. Mine was crushed indeed!

CHAPTER VI.

AFTER THE DELUGE.

OH, what dreadful days were those that succeeded this second great earthquake of the heart!

My dear father's death had made the once smiling past and the joyous present seem a very Golgotha, and now Roscommon's heartless desertion robbed the future of every ray of sunshine. It lay before me a black and dreary marsh, across which seemed to stretch a tortuous, narrow, uphill path, blocked up here and there by rugged stones, inter-

sected by dark and deep pools, and leading
on, on, on, to nothing but sandy deserts and
dreary wastes. The only symptoms of
vegetation seemed to my sad fancy to be
nettles, nightshade, and henbane; the only
trees and shrubs, yews, cypresses, rosemary,
and rue.

"Just such," I said to myself, "must
have been the wilderness into which the
angels with the flaming swords drove our
first parents."

They, like me, *had* dwelt in Eden. They,
like me, were driven out into the desert.

What then?

There is no soil so arid that it will not
yield some produce, ay, and some flowers,
in return for untiring labour.

Oh, weary fortune! Oh, lonely, dreary
wilderness! I must water thee with my
tears, and with the sweat of brow and brain.
I must redeem the arid soil, and force it to

yield at least a maintenance for my poor mother and myself.

And it was thus in truth. By degrees the dreadful reality dawned upon my mind. With my father we had lost everything. He had always lived up to the small income of his benefice. Hospitable as he was to his equals, and charitable in the extreme to the poor, the utmost my dear mother had done was, in common parlance, to make both ends meet.

Now, the question was, where were we to go? What were we to do?

I had not given a thought to our destitute and desolate condition—so absorbed was I by grief at my father's sudden and terrible death, and despair and humiliation at Roscommon's heartless desertion,—until a fresh burst of grief from old Bessie awakened my attention.

At that time my dear father had been one

month in his grave. The vicar of a neighbouring parish had officiated during that
time.

Now there was a change. The bells were
ringing merrily early on one sunny morning.

Bessie, whom I found, after vainly ringing for her, sitting by the kitchen fire, was
stopping her ears, rocking herself to and fro,
and moaning out, "Oh, them bells, them
bells! Oh, gineration of vipers! to go for to
ring like that 'ere, because a new minister's
coming to Moordell. They'll never see the
likes of him who's scarcely cauld in his
grave, as a body may say. Oh, them bells,
them bells! I heard 'em ring in my dear
dear master; little I thinked then I'd live
to hear them ring in another minister."

I understood from Bessie's ejaculations
that the bells were indeed ringing in the
new Vicar. He had been presented, it

seemed, soon after my father's death, by my uncle's son and heir, the Anglo-Indian youth, now Sir Selim Moore.

Of course, the new incumbent had not been chosen by Sir Selim or his mother; but they had influential friends in abundance now.

A county member had, it was said, paid assiduous court to Sir Selim, with the view of getting this living for a younger son, and the young baronet himself as a husband for his daughter.

The lady, however, was not to the young man's taste, but her brother was presented to the living of Moordell.

Soon after, my mother received the usual official communication. We had yet two months before us, and then we must quit the dear old Vicarage for ever!

As I said before, the question now was, where should we go? What should we do?

My mother's health was so delicate, and her nerves were so shattered, that I did not think it right or safe to moot this question before her, until I had come to some decision in my own mind. I felt it was my duty to live and work for my dear mother.

The past must be buried out of sight, and the arid present and the dark future must occupy all my thoughts.

I consulted with our dear, kind doctor, whose strong practical sense made him a very useful friend to me, and who offered me pecuniary help to carry out any plan I decided upon. Although his great charity to the poor of the parish had prevented his becoming rich, he had a modest competence.

The Count and the Signore shed many tears when I spoke to them of going into the cold, cold world, to earn a maintenance for my mother and myself.

The Signore being obliged to leave us to

attend a pupil at Warkworth, the Count remained some time standing at the window,
with his handkerchief to his eyes.   Suddenly
he came towards me, and tenderly embracing
me, said—

"*Ma petite! ma pauvrette!* You and
your dear moder" (he had never succeeded in
mastering the pronunciation of the *th*) "are
what I love best in de world, now he is
gone—de good, noble, Christian gentleman,
who was a broder to de exile.   I have
room, and to spare.   Come, your dear
moder and you, come and live wid me.   I
have enough for all our wants, and my
blessed moder's own room, of which I have
never made no use but to pray dere, since
she was taken from me: dat shall be de room
for your moder and you, *ma pauvrette!*"

I was very much affected at this proposal.
The Count was one of the most saving and
economical of men.   Ever since he had been

an exile he had practised the most rigorous self-denial. He made his own coffee, and attended to his *pot au feu*, in which the very smallest scrap of meat, with the herbs and vegetables which he cultivated himself in his own little garden, made a "*potage*" of which in childhood and early girlhood I had often partaken, and which was the very perfection of a *potage*, in the opinion of much better judges than myself—namely, my father and mother.

"*Façon de faire fait tout*," the dear old man would say, with a beaming smile, his black eyes glistening like jet beads, when my mother said that the Count's coffee, *potages*, and *omelettes* surpassed any to be met with even at the Castle.

" You know, *ma petite*," he said, resuming the conversation, "you know I am one good cook, and for you and your dear moder I will surpass myself; I will do prodiges;

I will do de impossible. Say, then, *ma pauvrette*, say you will come, and I will get ready my moder's room. She was one saint on eart'; she is one angel in heaven now; but you and your moder are wordy to inhabit her chamber. Say you will come, and we will be happy togeder."

I thanked him with tears rather than words, but I told him it could not be.

"I am strong, young, healthy," I said, "and I feel it is my duty to work for my mother and myself. I cannot do it here, it would wound her too much; but in London or some other great city."

"Oh, *ma pauvrette*," said the old man, weeping, "you know not what it is to work for hire. Oh, de world is so wicked where it pays—so spiteful, so cold!"

"I must bear it all, Count," I said, "as others have done before me."

"You look so pale, so changed, so ill," he

said; and then, with one of those sudden
bursts of passion which I had never seen in
him before, except when he spoke of the
Revolution, the martyrdom of his king and
queen, and some of the worst features of the
Reign of Terror, he cried, starting up, " Oh
dat I were one little bit parent to you, *ma
petite*, dat I might fight in a duel to de
deat' de false-hearted, base, money-loving,
fortune-hunting poltroon, who have rob your
heart of its peace, your life of its hope, your
cheek of its bloom ! He should not live to
see de ruin he have made; no, by heaven !
Oh, I would gladly shoot like a dog de
wretch who have deserted you, *ma petite*, in
your so great trouble. I cannot bear to tink
he live unpunished. Forgive me, it make
me mad. But see, here comes a fine coach.
Ha ! it is Mr. Fenwick. Oh, *ma petite*, if
he comes to offer hisself again, don't say
' No.' Tink of your moder, tink how dread-

ful to see her want. You see what heartless,
vain fellows young Englishmen are.   But
Mr. Fenwick dere is a fine man, of ripe age,
to sit by your side in a coach, to give you
his arm in a walk, to protect and to guide
you through life. Oh, *ma petite! ma pauvrette!*
tink of all dese tings, and don't say 'No.'
He is one good *parti.*"

" Don't go, Count," I cried.

" Two is company, and tree is none," he
cried. "Never will I be Monsieur de Trop;"
and, bowing with all the graceful courtesy
of the old school, the Count opened the glass
door that looked on to the lawn, and hurried
away.

CHAPTER VII.

FENWICK OF FENWICK AGAIN.

THE next moment Bessie announced Mr. Fenwick. He was in mourning. He looked very pale.

"I was in Italy, Miss Moore," he said, "when the terrible news reached me, or I should have been here long ago. I should have officiated as chief mourner, for none knew him better, or loved him more."

He walked to the window, and I saw that his gigantic frame was convulsed with emotion. He mastered it with a great effort, and coming to my side, he said, "How is your mother, Ada?" He was not in the habit of calling me Ada, and I started as I heard my name spoken by him.

"She is very ill," I said.

"We must remove her from this scene; it is fraught with torturing recollections to her, Ada," he resumed, and taking my hand. "It may seem premature, but I am only following the dictates of my heart and the counsels of my mind, in now renewing to you the offer I made you two months ago. I know all that has happened since then. I know, too, how ill your first choice was made, how basely your first love has been betrayed. I hope your experience of the falsehood, vanity, and cupidity of youth in Roscommon Lyall will make you appreciate the true and stable attachment of a middle-aged man. I do not wish to hurry you into matrimony, my child, but I do ask you to say you will one day be mine; and with that hope I will at once set about every possible arrangement for your mother's comfort, for I shall then look upon her as my mother. Say 'Yes,' Ada, and I will place Fenwick Park, and everything there, at your mother's disposal, and I will go away to London, and will not approach you until you yourself write to invite me to do so."

"Alas! I cannot accept your proffered kindness," I said, "for I cannot fulfil the conditions such acceptance entails,—I can never be your wife!"

"Why, what do you mean to do, Miss Moore?" he asked gruffly, and turning very red. "You cannot stay here! Mr. Lefevre has read himself in to-day. At the utmost, you cannot remain here more than a few weeks."

" I am aware of that, Sir," I said, rather proudly, for his roughness offended me.

" And where on earth are you going at the end of that time ? "

" To London," I replied.

"Why, what can you do there ?" he asked bitterly.

" I can turn my talents to account for my mother's support and my own," I said calmly.

" Stuff! nonsense! romance! The result of novel-reading! All heroines, nowadays, turn their talents to account, but in romance only. In reality they come to the Union. You little know what contempt, and even abuse, are showered on those very efforts, when taken into the market to be bartered for money, which secure such bravos, and excite such sham raptures, when exhibited *gratis*. Why, songs that are encored in a drawing-room would cause the singer to be hissed off the public stage. Drawings that are glazed and framed, and hung up and admired, at home, wouldn't fetch sixpence a dozen in the market. · You talk French and Italian well, very well for an English girl, thanks to the old French Count and the Italian Signore—what good will ˏthat do you ? Native professors are advertising lessons, in both these languages, at sixpence per hour. Ada, be advised! think of your mother !"

For a moment I was shaken, but my good angel whispered to my heart, " Can you love, honour, and obey this man ? If not, when you kneel at the altar by his side, you will blacken your soul with PERJURY !'"

He had taken my hand. I rent it from his grasp. I said firmly—

" Mr. Fenwick, it can never be ! I cannot love you, and I will never marry any man I cannot truly love ! "

His brow grew dark; a deep flush crimsoned his large face. He rose and said—

"Do not fear, Miss Moore, that I shall ever trouble you again on this subject, or on any other. Farewell for ever!"

As his sight was still very defective, I flew to get him his hat and his stick, and to ring the bell for his valet.

I offered him my hand at parting, but he either did not or would not see that I did so. His servant led him to his carriage, and he drove away.

"I have done right," I said to myself; and there was comfort in the thought, but my tears gushed forth as I thought of my mother. I told my mother,—for she had kept her room till the evening, the sound of the bells having greatly agitated her,— that Mr. Fenwick had renewed his proposals. I was distressed when she said—

"Oh, Ada! how I wish you *could* like him

well enough to accept him! How he, my beloved, wished it!"—and at the thought of *him*, her tears gushed forth.

I was vexed for a moment. Had I wronged my mother? I thought she was comparing the comforts of Fenwick Park with the penury that awaited her. But it was not so : she was not thinking of herself at all.

When I told her I could bear any privations, any sufferings, any amount of labour, better than such a marriage, and the perjury it would involve, she said she only wished I could love Mr. Fenwick, but that to marry him with the feelings I evidently had for him would be, in her opinion, a crime.

The days were getting shorter now, and we were in the habit of sitting in what had once been the most cheerful little breakfast-room in the world. It was hung with paintings of my mother's, etchings of my father's, and some old family portraits in pastils. There was a piano in that room once—it had been seldom shut, and now it was never opened.

There was a book-case of my parents' favourite authors—poems chiefly; stands of flowers, once marvels of freshness, beauty, and fragrance, because so tended and cared for, but now dying or dead; our work-boxes, and desks, and embroidery frames were there; in fact, all the evidences of home life and pleasant occupation. This room looked on the garden, and the gate that opened into the churchyard. We could see the old ivy-grown tower of our dear old church, and a few of the tall headstones so common in Northumberland.

It was under a grand old yew-tree, whose branches we could see from the windows of our little sitting-room, that my father lay; and when night closed in and Bessie brought lights and prepared to shut the shutters, the dreadful thought would force itself on my mind, as I could see it did on my mother's, —fantastic and foolish, but yet natural,—that we were shutting out my father from the fireside, of which he had ever been the pride and joy ; and when the autumnal night blast howled like a disconsolate spirit, and the rain pattered down, or the grey sea-fog clothed the whole landscape in half-mourning robes, the anguish of the thought that we were shutting in the light and warmth, and shutting him out for the rain to fall, the wind to moan, and the sea-fog to hide his resting-place from our view, was so intolerable, that when my mother was gone weeping to her room I have thrown open the shutters and the windows in a wild frenzy of grief; and, in spite of rain, wind, and fog, have hurried to his grave, with the silly thought that while his only child wept and knelt, and prayed, then he would be less alone.

Ah! in the first anguish of such bereavements, how vain is all that religion, reason, and philosophy can teach us of the utter nothingness of the frail tenement of clay upon the soul has fled! Still, of the earth earthy, the heart clings to the dear remains and never can divest itself of the idea that in the narrow grave the heart's darling lies asleep, awaiting the archangel's trump. And, after all, is it not so?

CHAPTER VIII.

ANOTHER CHANCE.

I HAD yet another strange chance of escape from the Battle of Life and the struggle for bare existence; but the conditions were quite as distasteful to me as a union with Fenwick of Fenwick would have been. The chance to which I allude was nothing less than a proposal from Sir Selim Moore. It was made through Mr. Goslyn, his solicitor, who said that the young gentleman had conceived so ardent a passion for me, child of the Sun as he was, on the one occasion

when we had met at the stile, that his peace
of mind, if not his life, depended on my
accepting his hand; that the ex-Begum, his
mother (Lady Moore), though at first much
opposed to the match, was now so tho-
roughly convinced of the intensity of her
son's attachment, and so very anxious about
its effect on his health, that she had resolved
to call on Mrs. Moore, and herself propose
the union.

" I strongly advise you, my dear young
lady," said Mr. Goslyn, "not to refuse an
offer which will secure to you the fine old
family property to which you were supposed
by every one (yourself, of course, included)
to be the heiress. You can make of Sir
Selim, loving you as he does, anything you
please; and he is munificently disposed as
far as settlements are concerned, and himself proposes that your mother should live
with you. But see, the Begum's palanquin

is at the gate. I have never seen her, for
she adheres to all Eastern customs, albeit
she is a Christian; therefore I will retire,
for mortal man must not gaze on the dark
and full-blown Venus of the East. Say
yes, and you are Lady Moore, of Moordell
Hall."

Mr. Goslyn hastily took his leave, and the
palanquin was carried by two black bearers
into the hall. Out rolled a very large, loose
figure wrapt in shawls—very rich shawls
indeed. She wore a turban and a linen veil,
so adjusted that nothing could be seen but
one large, sloping, sleepy black eye, very like
that of a ruminating cow. One of her female
attendants followed the ex-Begum, whom
Bessie ushered into our little morning-room,
which she absolutely seemed to fill. The attendant brought richly-embroidered cushions
out of the palanquin; and having placed
them on the floor, the ex-Begum reclined

among them, beckoning me to come and sit
by her.

She kissed me between my eyes, and expressed a wish for coffee and sweetmeats.

Bessie made some very good coffee, and I
brought out some boxes of French *bonbons*
which Roscommon had given me, and of
which she seemed to approve highly. After
this refreshment she began to smoke, and
almost to doze.

She was a very large woman, with jet
black hair and eyes and handsome features ;
but their beauty was destroyed by the super-
abundance of flesh, that made her cheeks
and chin appear monstrous, and her form
shapeless and unwieldy.

She spoke broken English, and, as far as
I can remember, she said, " My son, Sir
Selim Moore, by birth Prince of ——, have
cast on you, maiden, the eye of love. He
wish to take you to wife. And like as

Sarah was to Abraham, and Rebecca to Isaac, and Rachel to Jacob, and so many more holy women of old to their lords and masters, so I hope you will be a wife dutiful and loving to my son. He is sick for love of you; you can rejoice his soul if you say kind words to him and promise to be his true and loving wife."

I told the Begum I was much flattered and felt highly honoured, but I must decline her gracious proposal and Sir Selim's offer.

At first she laughed incredulously; but when convinced that I was in earnest, she became very angry, and to my great relief she rose frowning and in silence, and with the help of her attendant rolled back into her palanquin and was conveyed away to the Hall.

It was only on the Moordell estate that she went about in a palanquin; but she considered herself a sort of absolute monarch

of Moordell, and that she could do just as
she pleased.

I was very sorry that Sir Selim had taken
this useless fancy for me, but I looked upon
him as a sort of Indian juggler or Hindoo
acrobat; and the idea of marrying such a
creature seemed to me too absurd for me to
dwell upon it for a moment.

After these two breaks in the mournful
monotony of our existence, we went on very
quietly. The Count still urged our acceptance of his offer, and the Signore was full of
a scheme for joining Garibaldi, and for the
ultimate regeneration of Italy.

CHAPTER IX.

MY PRAYER IS ANSWERED.

I was with many tears making gradual and quiet preparations for leaving our dear home.

I had had a visit from Mr. Lefevre, the new Vicar, and he had seemed to me a very amiable and sympathizing young man. He was newly married, and, of course, as he was living in rather inconvenient lodgings in the village, he was anxious to take possession of the Vicarage. But with great tact and delicacy he concealed that fact.

We had still, by law or rather custom, a

right to remain six weeks longer; and my
mother's convalescence was so very gradual,
I thought she would not be fit to move in a
shorter time.

There is generally in all great sorrows a
merciful dispensation, whereby we are spared
some minor, but yet very keen, distresses.

It was so with us, in one respect. Mr.
Lefevre wished to take our furniture at a
valuation, and we felt that thus we should be
spared all the heart-rending mortification of
a sale.

Our household gods would not be dragged
from their shrine, to be put up for sale, and,
after countless ribald jests, to be knocked
down to the highest bidder. This was an
unspeakable comfort to me. I had so dreaded
the sale, and the thought of it was worm-
wood to old Bessie : she could not patiently
endure the idea that the furniture, and still
more the kitchen utensils, in which for more

than twenty years she had taken so much
pride, should pass into other hands, "maybe to be niglicted and misprized," as she
said. But even that was a small grief compared to the dread of having them "jeered at
and sneered at in the open air, by that ne'er-
do-weel of a fellow, the auctioneer fra Alnwick, wha would mak a jest o' his mother's
coffin, if he could turn a shilling thereby."

I had almost decided in my own mind,—
that was, if my mother did not object,—that
as soon as our now fast-expiring month of
grace at the Vicarge was ended, and the
furniture paid for, we should go to London,
take a cheap and quiet lodging, and that I
should at once endeavour to obtain employment as a daily governess.

It was a dreary and a painful prospect.
I saw, however, no other by which I could
make tolerably sure of enough for my mother
and myself to live on.

This plan of mine, however, was not destined to be carried into execution, and I cannot say that I regretted it ; for though I had nerved myself to contemplate, with a sort of satisfaction, the labour, the hardships, the sacrifice of ease, pride, and comfort which my new career must involve, I could not guise from myself that my mother's very delicate health would, in all probability, suffer from the long lonely hours she would have to spend daily in some close London lodging, and at the thought of what her life would necessarily be under such circumstances. The fortitude which had not forsaken me when I contemplated my own altered fortunes, vanished when I thought of hers, and I asked myself in anguish and perplexity, "What else can I do?"

CHAPTER X.

A FAIRER PROSPECT.

And, lo! in answer to that question came a better and a fairer prospect.

It unfolded itself in the shape of a letter from the Duchess of Northlands· to my mother. The substance of this letter, which was written in the kindest and most amiable spirit possible, was to the effect that Lady Beatrice, her niece, having been ordered by her doctors to winter at Mentone, and having no female relative or lady friend with whom she could travel and reside, and Dr. Dartmoor having said that nothing would do

so much towards the restoration of the health
and spirits of Mrs. and Miss Moore as a
winter in the South of France, she, the
Duchess, had decided on asking my mother
to undertake the chaperonage of the young
lady, who was overjoyed at the thought of
her friend Ada's companionship, and that,
in return for the inestimable advantage to
Beatrice of such a chaperon and such a
companion, all expenses would be gladly de-
frayed by Lord Mountjoy, Lady Beatrice's
father.

The Duchess added, that should it please
God to bless this change, and to restore
Beatrice to health, it was then in' contemplation, with Mrs. Moore's acquiescence, that
on the same terms, when the South became
too hot, Beatrice should visit the German
Spas, and spend the succeeding winter in
Italy, by which time it was hoped that her
strength might be quite restored, and that

she might then be able (that was to say, at
·the end of two years) to return to England,
to be presented, and to take her place as
mistress of her father's establishment.

Nothing could exceed the kindness, the
delicacy, the tact, and the sympathy with
which the Duchess conveyed to my mother
that the pecuniary arrangements would be of
the most liberal nature, and that letters of
credit in her name would secure any funds
she might require in any Continental towns
she visited.

Carte blanche was offered to my dear
mother, as to all arrangements; but the
Duchess suggested, as likely to save time and
fatigue to Beatrice and ourselves, that Lord
Deville's yacht should convey us to Nice,
and that we should set out in a fortnight's
time, as that would bring us to the end of
November.

"What say you, my Ada?" asked my

mother, when she had read this kind letter herself and had given me time to peruse it.

I looked up; my mother's eyes were gazing through these leaves at the yew-tree beneath which my father lay. I saw, as plainly as if she had bared her poor widowed heart, that hope and happiness, and all real interest in life, as far as she was concerned, were buried there, and that the first idea suggested by the Duchess's letter was, "I must leave him there. I must go far, far away from him. I may die in that distant land they wish me to go to, and be buried far away from him."

My mother had now reached that age when Fear rather than Hope is the heart's prophet. It was not so with me. I was almost ashamed—I, so recently deprived of such a father—to find joy gush into my heart like sunshine at the thought of this delicious prospect.

I had always so longed to see Mentone.

The Signore's mother had been a Mentonese lady. He had passed his boyhood amid the magic beauties of that enchanted spot. From my infancy he had talked to me of the Riviera, and delighted me with the legends which had been told him by his old Mentonese nurse. I knew all the ghastliest ghost stories, the histories of the old families and their castles. I had by heart the names of the modern tyrants of the simple and generous Mentonese, and had learnt from the Signore to couple Honorius V. with the worst of the Roman emperors, and to glow at the history of the brave resistance of the people, and the final overthrow of the oppressor. The Signore's portfolio was full of spirited water-colour paintings of the most beautiful scenes, where all was beauty. I had copied many of them under his guidance, and now I was to see them. I was to climb those olive-clad hills. I was to breathe

that sunny air, fragrant with the scent of a
thousand flowers ; to gather the oranges and
lemons, ripe and fresh from the trees; to
hear the *patois* the Signore spoke so well;
perhaps to see that Christian heroine, Mdlle.
Lenoir, of whom he never spoke without
emotion. Of course, in the solemn presence
of my mother's holy grief, I could not speak
of the solace this new prospect promised me.
What was all the scenery of the Riviera to
one who felt no interest in any spot on
earth, but that where her beloved lay ? I
almost hated myself, as hard and unnatural,
for being able so soon to think with a glow
of pleasure of Dolceaqua, Ventimiglia, and
Bordighera, Turbia, Laghetto, and Esu,
Monaco, Il Gran Mondo, Beglia, Castiglione,
Ghiandola, and many other places which the
Signore's spirited pencil and eloquent tongue
had made me familiar with, and which, from
my very earliest days, it had been my hope
and my dream to behold.

After a silence of some minutes, my mother said, " Ada, you must answer this letter, and decide this question. I am too much unnerved to be capable of a resolution. But I feel—I suppose—we ought to accept."

She wept bitterly as she said so, and hurried out into the garden, and thence into the churchyard. Dear, desolate mother! Poor mourning widow! My heart bled for her, but I felt that the best thing for her was change, and such a change.

Already the sea fogs enveloped Moordell like a blanket. Already the cold north wind made the fir-trees bow and quail and groan before its irresistible but invisible presence. Already snow was beginning to fall, and winter to set in. Winter at Moordell, and my father in his grave! It seemed to me impossible but that, were we to remain, the late spring of the north would find my mother by his side.

I gratefully accepted, for my mother and myself, the Duchess's most kind and generous proposal; and now, with only a fortnight before me for every preparation, I was obliged to exert myself; and active employment is among the best cures for the heart-ache.

CHAPTER XI.

THE TESTIMONIAL.

DURING this last fortnight of our stay at Moordell many little incidents occurred, which to my mother and myself were very affecting. The one was the presentation to my mother and myself of a testimonial, which it had been long in contemplation to offer to my father. For some years a subscription had been going on among the poor of the parish, the object of which was to show their love and reverence for their pastor in the shape of a piece of plate. But, car-

nest as was their desire, they were so few in
number, and so poor, that it had taken a
long time to amass a sum sufficient for their
grateful and generous purpose. Two or
three wealthy farmers had, however, con-
tributed liberally; and at length a silver
coffee-pot, tea-pot, cream jug, and sugar
basin were decided upon and purchased.

It was a general holiday in the parish,
was that day on which the testimonial was
to be presented. The village school-room
was to be the scene of the presentation, and
the new Vicar was to officiate. I much
feared that my dear mother would not be
equal to the painful excitement of such a
ceremony, and I tried to dissuade her from
being present; but I found she had quite
made up her mind to receive this touching
tribute to my dear father in person, as the
best return she could make for the years of
faithful love, gratitude, and self-denial which

such a testimonial from such a parish in-
volved.

She had been latterly so very weak, nervous, and hysterical, that her firmness and
resolution astonished me. The secret of it
was, that she felt as if she had yet something
to do to show her devotion to my father, and
her love for his flock.

At one o'clock the Count and the Signore,
both subscribers, came to escort us to the
school-house. My mother was very pale,
and her deep widow's mourning made her
look all the more so. I thought a sculptor
could have chosen no finer model for a marble
statue of widowed love.

All the village was assembled: from the
oldest inhabitant (in a country famous for
longevity) down to babes in arms, no one
not bed-ridden was absent; and my tears
overflowed when I saw that every one had
contrived to put on some evidence of mourn-

ing. A black ribbon, brown with time, bound the white caps of old, grey-headed women, to whom the braw Vicar had seemed so hale and young. A bit of rusty crape had been found for every hat, which was respectfully doffed as my mother made her appearance. The whole scene was intensely exciting and painfully agitating; but she bore it bravely.

I saw her eyes grow unnaturally bright, and a pink spot deepens on her alabaster cheek. I was aware that she trembled with emotion, but to my surprise I saw she mastered it.

On a table in the centre of the school-room was the testimonial, covered with a white cloth; and when my mother and I were seated, the Rev. Mr. Lefevre, in a short speech, replete with good taste and good feeling, having uncovered it, offered it to my mother and myself in the name of the grateful congregation of a late devoted minister. He then read the inscription, which was engraved on each article, and which, he said, would convey far better than he could the feelings of the subscribers:—

"To the Wife and Daughter of their late beloved, lamented, and devoted Pastor, the Rev. Edmond Moore, Vicar of Moordell; the flock he tended with so wise and tender a zeal for more than twenty years, presents the tribute which, originally intended for himself, is now offered to his venerated memory and to those he loved best on earth."

My mother's forced composure gave way completely before the touching sympathy of this inscription. She tried to speak, but sobs choked her utterance. She turned to the Count, as if to bid him to speak for her. The old man started up and said—

"Dear friends, she tank you. De wife tank you, de widow tank you; de child, de

only child of him who is no dere," he said,
pointing to the churchyard, " but *dere*," and
he raised his eyes and hands to heaven,
"tank you. He may be present here—at
least his blessed spirit, I tink he is; but
spirits cannot speak, and so I speak for him
when I say, tousand tousand tanks! Tank
one, tank all! Amen."

Very beautiful and bright, of a chaste
pattern, and in the best possible taste, was
the silver service, as it shone in the noonday
sun, surrounded by a wreath which must
have robbed the cottage gardens of Moordell
of all their late flowers. Every one wept;
for every one thought of him who for more
than twenty years had filled that chair in
which the new Vicar now sat.

As my mother's agitation was becoming
very great, the old Count offered his arm to
lead her from the scene. The Signore gave
me his, and, after shaking hands with all

assembled in the school-room, we returned to the Vicarage.

Another touching incident was the arrival of a letter from Harry Blake, enclosing, with words of the deepest sympathy and respect, a hundred pound note, "as a very, very small instalment," he said, "of that great debt he owed to his beloved patron and friend, to whom he was indebted for everything he possessed, or was ever likely to possess, on earth." He was staying at Palermo, he said, with a pupil whose lungs were delicate, and added that, had he been free, he should have placed himself at my mother's disposal, too proud if she had condescended to make any use of the creature of her beloved husband's bounty.

Mrs. Hodgson had written several times to condole with us since our dreadful bereavement. She had said that she had many secret sorrows of her own, and that at some future time she hoped to pour them unto my mother's sympathizing heart and ear, and that she bitterly regretted not having followed her advice in the first instance. Evil, she said, had already come of the deception Smithkin had forced her to practise, and she feared worse was in store for her.

I wrote to tell her that we were going to the South for some time, and to thank her for her sympathy with us in our unspeakable bereavement.

CHAPTER XII.

THE DEATH OF HOPE.

A few days before we were to set out, a
newspaper, the ' Morning Post,' came directed to me. I knew the hand. It was
that of Smithkin Hodgson. It contained a
brilliant account of the marriage, at St.
George's, Hanover Square, of — of — Roscommon Lyall, Esq., to Margaretta Ann,
third daughter of Joseph Hodgson, Esq., of
Berkeley Square. The Brussels lace, the
white satin, the orange flowers, and the
pearls of the bride, together with the mauve

silks, ribbon wreaths, and tulle veils of the
bridesmaids, seemed to float in a sort of
chaos before my eyes. A spasm contracted
my heart. The paper fell from my hand,
and, for some minutes, consciousness forsook
me. I did not know, myself, that I still
cared so much for that false, heartless de-
ceiver; but we seldom do gauge the depth of
our affections, and can only judge of them ourselves by their effects. It was, of course, in a
spirit of paltry revenge that Smithkin had
sent me the paper, but it did me good in the
end. Withering contempt supplied the place
of any lingering tenderness that yet lurked
in my heart; and when I remembered how
Roscommon had ridiculed the very woman
he had now sworn to love and cherish for
ever, I saw him as he was—a sordid fortune-hunter! I despised him; and love,
which may exist for a despicable object,
never can endure for one that is despised.

* * * * *

"Bessie," I said, two days before we were to quit Moordell,—"dear, good old Bessie! what do you mean to do? Whither do you mean to go when we have left Moordell?"

. "Weel, and that is a strange question, Miss Ada!" said Bessie. "I dinna think your mither would put it til me. What will I du, and whither will I gang? Why I'll du as I've dune these twa and twenty year, my bairnie,—I'll wait on the Missus and yersel', night and day, hond and fute; and I'll follow ye baith to the warld's end, and where ye dwell I'll dwell, and your hame shall be my hame!"

Bessie had made up her mind to follow us, and, on the whole, we were glad to have the faithful creature with us. She was a quaint, curious, wonderful old creature, in her blue flannel gown and white linen cap and apron, to take to the South; but what matter, as she said—

" If I'm to believe the Signore's drawings, and the prints in the travel bukes, I'll see queerer figures nor I be, and more or'nary faces too; and if they stare and speer at me, I've give as gude as I tak, and there'll be na love lost between us, I con tell ye, Miss Ada !"

The last morning came, dull and drizzly. The sun was wrapt in mist and sea fog. The fly was at the gate, to carry us to the station. The luggage had preceded us thither. The Count and the Signore went with us inside; Bessie was on the box. At the end of the lane we found all the parish assembled to wish us 'God speed;' and amid tears, fare-wells, blessings, and the waving of hats, handkerchiefs, and hands, we drove to the station.

The Signore told me, as we parted, "We

may meet soon, for I hope to join Garibaldi in a few months."

The Count, who had brought Mignon with him in his bosom, held the beautiful bird on his forefinger, first to my mother and then to me; and the intelligent creature, as if aware that we were going, kissed our lips with his ebon beak, and then fluttered back to the old Count's bosom, screeching, '*Vive le Roi!*' He put a small box into my hand, and embraced my mother and myself fervently.

As the train rushed off with us along the shining rails, I saw the old Count weeping bitterly in the Signore's arms.

CHAPTER XIII.

SAD HEARTS AND THE SAD SEA WAVES.

I SHALL pass briefly over our voyage, although it seemed very long, monotonous, and tedious to us all.

I may as well mention here that, as soon as I had an opportunity of doing so in private, I opened the little box the dear old Count had put into my hand at parting.

I could not repress my tears when I saw that the box contained his diamond ring and his diamond brooch! I knew how dearly he prized these relics of the past—

these remnants of former grandeur—and I felt, deeply felt, the sacrifice he had made in parting with them.

In his own elegant and classical French—the French of the *Vieille Cour*—he had written a few lines, the purport of which was as follows :—

" I always meant to bequeath these jewels to your father, *ma pauvrette.* He was my best and dearest friend. I now give them to you, to be converted into money if you are ever in want. Great people are fickle ; Lady Beatrice may leave you or she may die. But wherever you are, these diamonds will fetch their price.

" Your all-devoted old friend,

" ALCESTE DE MORTEMER."

* * * * *

A sea voyage has often proved efficacious to those suffering from diseases of the lungs ; but to those afflicted with grief—that greatest of mental maladies—and with the fever of vain longing for those gone for ever, the confinement of a cabin and the monotony of the ocean are very trying.

Lady Beatrice was ill and dejected ; my poor mother could not bear up at all. The thought of a world of waters rolling between her and her adored one added to her grief.

There is such a tendency to musing as we watch the endless rolling of the waves, and to us thought was torture.

Ere long, although it was very calm when we embarked, the wind rose, and the yacht laboured and tossed, and rose and sank ; and, for a time, even mental anguish was swamped in the unutterable suffering, pain, and distress caused by sea-sickness.

Poor Bessie was always wishing herself "bock at Moordell—or even at the bottom o' the say !"

The weather continued so rough—or, as

the sailors called it, so " dusty "—that companionship was impossible. We none of us could leave our berths or hold up our heads.

Lord Deville, Beatrice's cousin, was a gloomy, silent man, disappointed as a statesman, and who, having been jilted by the woman he loved, disliked women in general and young ladies in particular. Still everything that could be done to mitigate our really intense suffering was done.

We had every attention, every comfort; but we could appreciate nothing, enjoy nothing; and the only gleam of comfort that cheered us was the news—after a fortnight of restless tossing on the waves—that Nice was in sight. We thought it an age from the time we received that intelligence till we reached the harbour. We were so exhausted by a fortnight of suffering unutterable, we had to be carried to the nearest hotel.

Oh! the unspeakable comfort of finding oneself on *terra firma* after the swaying and swinging, the heaving and diving of fourteen days and nights!

My dear mother, Lady Beatrice, and poor old Bessie were unable to leave their beds for three days and nights.

Lady Beatrice's cough was very troublesome, and her sufferings during the voyage had greatly increased the fever and nightly perspirations attendant on her disease.

I felt perfectly well and strong after one night's rest; and when I rose on the first morning of our stay at Nice, after twelve hours of sound sleep, and looked from my window on the beautiful bay, sparkling—although it was December—in just such a sun as we see in May in England, and felt the warm breeze that came in, laden with the fragrance of orange flowers, violets, and musk roses, I felt for the first time that

there are climates in which existence itself
is a luxury, and the very air at once an
elixir and a balm.

On the third day from that of our landing
at Nice, my mother, old Bessie, and even
Lady Beatrice felt equal to resuming our
journey; and as the Duchess of Northlands
had impressed on my mother and myself the
importance of reaching Mentone as soon as
possible, we postponed the pleasure of lionizing Nice to some future opportunity; and
apartments had been secured for us by Mr.
W——, the English grocer at Mentone, to
whom I had written by the advice of our
landlord at Nice.

It was rather late in the day when we left
beautiful Nice in a vetturino carriage; my
mother, Lady Beatrice, and myself inside;
Bessie, and Lady Beatrice's fine lady's-
maid, Proudfoot, in a sort of rumble, at
which, dirty and quaint as it certainly was,

Proudfoot would have turned up her nose, had not nature saved her that trouble.

Bessie, who had all a Borderer's dignity and sense of her own importance, was not at all awed or cowed by Proudfoot's airs.

On the contrary, on the principle of *seniores priores,* she now took the lead and the best, where there was a choice, in everything appropriated to the two attendants. This she explained to me, in her own quaint way, as follows :—

" Ye ken weel eneugh, Miss Ada, that I'm mair for ithers than for my ain sel'; that's my principle, and was that o' my mither afore me; and when first Proudfute cam amang us I gev her the choice in a' things, and waited on her hond and fute. But I sune saw that I was in the wrang box a'thegither, for she began to toss her head, and brag, and boast, and talk fine, and trate me like a Turk. And ain day she said to

me, 'Ye'll please to ca' me Miss Proudfute,
auld woman'!"

"'Deed will I," I replied, "but ainly when
you ca' me Miss Bessie. We're nathing
mair nor less than twa paid serving lasses,
Proudfute—aquals in a' respects, saving that
as I'm maybe a trifle the elder o' the twa,
I tak precedence in a' things. I ha'na dune
sae hitherto out of gude nature; but hence-
forth I'll keep my place and expect you to
do the same; and if ye want respeck and
ceeveelity fra me, ye'll ha' to show the same
til me, and that's a' aboot it."

This spirited self-assertion of Old Bessie's
had made some impression on Proudfoot. All
Bessie's unselfish kindness had only made
Proudfoot insolent and overbearing; but
now she respected the quaint old Borderer,
for she had learnt that she could only secure
respect from Bessie by treating her politely.

This point settled, they became pretty

good friends, and were much more lively and
merry in the rumble than we were in the inside of the carriage.

Bessie had quite recovered her health and
spirits. She had been extremely distressed,
and even convulsed with grief, during the first
few weeks after my dear father's sudden and
violent death ; but to mourn long, and, like
my poor mother, with greater intensity as
time goes by, you must belong to the thinking, the educated classes.

The first terrible shock and ghastly impression which the death of the loved makes
on the senses over, the unimaginative, unre-
flecting, and unrefined, easily reconcile themselves to the irremediable, the irrevocable.

Wise in their simplicity, they say, "It
was God's will ; the tears of the living do
no good to the dead. We must all die ; we
shall soon follow ; we believe he's better
off; and it is our duty to say, ' The Lord

gave, and the Lord taketh away; Blessed be the name of the Lord. Thy will be done.'"

Thus it was with Bessie; and she blamed my mother and myself for our pale cheeks, heavy eyes, and persistency in that unavailing regret, that morbid remorse, that fever of vain longing, which belong to those accustomed to think,—ingenious self-tormentors, whose own imaginations and over-sensitive consciences doom them to tortures more protracted and agonizing to the mind than the Inquisition ever inflicted on the body.

We were indeed a mournful trio inside the *vettura*. Lady Beatrice, ill and low-spirited, probably felt depressed by our despondency, and missed the comforts of England without having as yet enjoyed any of the beauties of scenery and climate she had expected to find in the South. My mother and myself, in our deep mourning and deep grief, were not exactly the best companions

for the young invalid. The sun, on whose
tremendous power all the warmth and brilliancy of the climate of Nice depends, had
not shone out to dissipate a thick mist or
sea-fog, which, before we reached the summit
of the Turbette, had begun to melt into very
fine drizzling rain.

I felt it to be an imperative duty to try
to rouse myself, to endeavour to cheer and
amuse Lady Beatrice. She was a sweet,
gentle creature, but intelligent withal. I
think she saw the effort I was making, and
understood and appreciated my motive, for
she placed her thin burning hand in mine.

"Don't exert yourself to talk for my sake.
In sorrow it is so much more pleasant to be
silent. I can amuse myself with my own
thoughts; or, if they are barren or dull, I
have 'Dr. Antonio' in my bag."

Here was a pleasant and suggestive subject for discussion.

We had both read that interesting work, but differed in opinion about Lucy. Lady Beatrice admired her timid, submissive character and her sacrifice of self, and all the warm impulses of her young heart in marrying Lord Cleverton, whom she did not love, to please a tyrant, coarse-minded brother, and to conform to the conventionalities of a cold world.

I maintained that Lucy had no right to marry Lord Cleverton when her heart was devoted to Dr. Antonio,—that it was cowardice, and that as one fault always brings others in its train, so Lucy's cowardice brought with it cruelty and ingratitude to Antonio, and, finally, blackened her own soul with perjury.

We were discussing Lucy's conduct—I warmly accusing and Lady Beatrice faintly defending her—when a cry escaped her lips. She caught me by the arm. It was almost

dark, but yet she could see that we were
galloping along the ledges of the Turbette,
and were, in fact, at the very edge of a
frightful precipice, just as darkness began to
close in.

Beatrice held me tightly by the arm till
we reached the plain, when she exclaimed,
" Thank heaven we are safe !" but just as
she spoke those words the carriage suddenly
stopped, and the driver shouted out, " *Les
Eaux ! Les Eaux !*"

We had been told at Nice that we should
have frightful precipices to encounter, and to
pass " *Les Eaux* "—very much swollen, as
they would be, by recent rains. We had,
however, no idea of what this danger would
really be, until, by the light of a few faintly
twinkling stars, we saw a miniature Niagara
foaming and rushing across the road ; and
while Proudfoot screamed and Bessie scolded,
the driver shouted out that we must all alight

and wade through Les Eaux on foot, for that
the carriage could not cross Les Eaux with
us in it.   Here was a terrible dilemma !   It
was raining, and though to me individu-
ally it mattered very little, for I had been
used in dear old Northumberland to ford
streams, yet I dreaded it for my still very
delicate mother, and for the invalid Lady
Beatrice.   What might not be the result of
their being wetted to the skin by the rain,
and of their being obliged to wade more
than ankle-deep through the torrent ?

I was expostulating with the driver on
the subject, when fortunately another carriage drove up close behind our own.   Two
gentlemen alighted, and approached.   They
very politely offered their services.   One of
them was a very tall, strong, middle-aged Englishman, fair, florid, handsome, and military-
looking.   His companion was a Mentonese—
M. de Monleon, a very interesting, and even

poetical-looking young man,. with very dark
eyes and hair, and the sort of head Rem-
brandt would have given to a youthful saint
and martyr.

The Englishman introduced himself as
Colonel Ridley.   It was a Northumbrian
name.   My mother had known some of his
family.   He offered to carry her to a little
foot-bridge, which, near at hand, rose above
the water.   He had a plaid, which he insisted on throwing round my mother.   With
his help she safely crossed the foot-bridge,
and met the carriage, which had been driven
round through the stream higher up.   M. de
Monleon insisted on Lady Beatrice's accepting a similar service from him.   It was of
course more embarrassing for a girl to allow
a handsome young stranger to take her in
his arms, than for my mother to avail herself of the help of a middle-aged country-
man, whose family she had known; but

Beatrice, though exquisitely modest and reserved, was no prude. She saw she was
keeping M. de Monleon and myself standing in shallows while the rain was pouring
down upon us, and so she suffered him to
throw his martial cloak around her, and to
bear her to the foot-bridge, along which,
with his help, she proceeded until she
reached the carriage. Our new friends there
took their leave, expressing a hope of seeing
us again soon, and Colonel Ridley, offering
his hand to my mother, said—

"I am at Mentone for the sake of my only
girl, the last of five left me by my dear wife,
who died of consumption while they were all
little children. Whether we shall save my
poor Violet or not, no one, not even the
doctor, can tell; but she has rallied a good
deal since she came to Mentone."

"I hope we shall have the pleasure of
seeing her," said my mother, giving the

I 2

Colonel our address, and then the two gentle-
men took their leave.

I remember that Lady Beatrice blushed
deeply as she bowed, and smilingly thanked
M. de Monleon for the service he had ren-
dered her, and the olive cheek of the handsome stranger crimsoned as his dark glances
met her soft blue eyes.

And thus having passed safely through
the great dangers of the precipices and " Les
Eaux," we perceived lights shining through
a haze, and a narrow street looming in the
distance, and the driver shouted out that we
had reached Mentone. It was not, however,
without considerable difficulty that we found
the house in which our apartments were
situated.

The " Nice " driver seemed to know nothing at all of the geography of Mentone.
We were obliged to drive on in the dark,
stopping now and then to question a foot

passenger, who, too good-natured to own he did not know the Maison Grimaldi, misled us by directions which took us out of the way. We could see lights in some of the curious old buildings above us, so high up that they looked like stars. We could hear the roaring of the sea, but we were beginning to despair of finding our future home, when an English servant, luckily perceiving our dilemma from the doorway of a house he was entering, came up and gave the driver such lucid directions in his own patois, that even he, stolid and stupid as he was, could not make any more mistakes, and we reached the Maison Grimaldi, very thankful to be home at last.

When we entered the house, a strong and exquisite odour of lemon and orange blossoms and of jasmine seemed to welcome us to our new home; and as we entered our bright and pleasant drawing-room on the first floor,

we saw large bouquets of these flowers on
the tables, yet it was December 14. We
were too weary that night to do more than
retire to our bedrooms, Bessie undertaking
to bring us tea, and any other refreshment
she could procure.

Two native maid-servants had been in-
stalled, ready to receive us and wait on us;
and, with their good-humoured help and
Bessie's zeal, some very good tea, rolls, eggs,
and a broiled chicken, were got ready;
Proudfoot sneering and scowling the while,
and declaring she could never enjoy her tea
without cream and butter. There was a
small supply of sheep's milk, but butter
there was none. Lucia, one of the maids,
explained that all the butter obtained at
Mentone came from Milan, and that when
the passage called the Col di Tenda was
snowed up, as it had been for the last few
days, the Queen of England herself could

not have got any butter at Mentone. Proudfoot, seeing there was no help for it, wisely
followed Bessie's advice to "mak the best o'
it, and tak wha' she could get and be thankfu';" and Proudfoot did so, except as far as
the last clause was concerned.

CHAPTER XIV.

BEAUTIFUL MENTONE.

THE bright sun of the South came, betimes, into our pleasant rooms on the first morning of our abode at Mentone.

December by the calendar,—June by the atmosphere, the flowers, and our feelings. It was St. Benoît's Day, and St. Benoît is the St. Swithin of Mentone,—just as false and faithless as our own St. Swithin, but yet as firmly believed in. Lucia told me with confidence, that we might make sure of forty days of fine weather if it did not rain on St. Benoît's Day.

The sunny-faced, dark-eyed, merry Mentonese Lucia gave me this good news when she came into my room early, to offer her services at my toilet. As far as I could understand, from a few words of French mixed with her own curious but not unmusical patois, the old Camericra, Bessie, was waiting on La Padrona (my mother), and La Superba, as she laughingly called Proudfoot, was in attendance on the Signorina (Lady Beatrice). She, therefore, proposed to instal herself as my Abigail; and her bright scarlet lips smiled so sweetly and disclosed such beautiful white teeth, and her voice was so sweet, and her manners so engaging, that, although I soon discovered that she knew nothing of the duties of a lady's-maid, yet I was very glad to have so pleasant and picturesque a creature, at any rate trying to help me. And yet it was a *trial* on both sides, for Lucia insisted on brushing my hair, the unwonted colour of which (golden, as she would have it), so rare in the South, delighted her, and the agony she caused me sent the tears to my eyes. She seemed to me to be pulling my whole *chevelure* up by the roots, and yet praising my hair and her own skill all the time. I could not bear it, and turning up my tresses, asked her to lace my dress. She missed several holes, and laughed so prettily at her blunders, I could not scold her.

When she had unpacked my trunk, and done wonders, according to her own notion, as I found from her self-laudatory ejaculations, she left me, and I sprang from my snow-white bed and hurried to my window to see what Mentone was really like.

Never shall I forget the overpowering sensation of rapture, admiration, and the overwhelming sense of the grand and the beautiful, as my eyes wandered from groves, magnificent olive-trees, and gardens, where flowers of every lovely form and hue emitted fragrance of every exquisite variety—to a vast expanse of sea of a translucent cobalt blue ! The peaks of a mountain (which I afterwards learnt was the Berceau) rose, in the distance, from among groves of orange and lemon trees, and a chain of rocks of a lovely rose colour, many of them precipitous, girded the azure waters of the Bay.

Oh for the brush of Turner, of Claude Lorraine, and of Salvator Rosa, to convey a faint idea of the beauties of that landscape ! Turner, at his best, could alone have portrayed the sunny, semi-transparent haze—the soft veil through which Nature's face looked all the fairer. He alone could have fixed on canvas the fleeting fairy vision of Corsica, when, at sunrise, you see her across the deep blue sea, and, by that magic rosy light, trace every fissure, and every crag, ravine,

and projection, and almost conjure up, by the
force of fancy and association, that little
island's great boast—*le petit Caporal*, standing, as in one of Turner's pictures he does
stand, with folded arms, and pale contracted
brow, upon a rocky coast, looking across the
world of waters!   That rocky coast was the
coast of St. Helena!

Strange fate!

Born on the rocky isle of Corsica to conquer all the world, save our brave little
island, and, for aiming at that, to die at St.
Helena!

Hours together I have stood at my bedroom window at Mentone, gazing at Corsica
by sunrise, when it seemed so near, that I
fancied I could row myself over to its rocky
shore, if I had a boat at my command, and
pondering, as I gazed at Napoleon Bona-
parte's birthplace, on the wondrous history
of his career, seeing, with my mind's eye,

the hero boy at college, playing at soldiers, at taking and defending fortresses, at leading forlorn hopes—practising, in childhood, the daring policy, the sublime inscrutability, the prompt, all-daring seizure of opportunity, which made him, in due time, the master of Europe ; flinging, with disdainful hand, the crowns he had seized to tributary kings.

As I gazed at Corsica, with my mind's eye, I saw Josephine, assistant architect of his great fortunes, his friend when he was friendless, his devoted, faithful wife,—I saw her, in his proudest hour, repudiated, forsaken, humbled, and in tears. I saw a cold blonde image take the place of that warm, woman-hearted, bright, gifted Josephine ; and I traced, through Napoleon's after story, his downfall and his destruction, to his cruel ingratitude to Josephine—his perjury and desertion !

Often, at evening, I gazed from the same

window at Corsica, where, white and misty
as the ghost of the great Napoleon himself,
it looms in the distance, and seems lost in the
clouds, far, far away.

But I must call home my thoughts from
Napoleon and the past, to record the events of
our first day at beautiful Mentone, and to
state what were our first impressions of that
quaint and lovely spot. When we met at
breakfast in our *salle à manger*—a dull room
when compared with our two bright draw-
ing-rooms and cheerful bed-rooms—I saw
that my dear mother looked pale and depressed, and that her eyes were red and
swollen with weeping.

Bessie told me afterwards that when first
my mother gazed as I had done, entranced,
enraptured at the glorious view from her
window, similar to that I had so enjoyed from
mine, she heard her say, as the tears gushed
from her eyes, "And all this wondrous

beauty has been lying here since the world began, and *he* never saw it ! And while I am breathing this balmy air, and while the warm sun cheers and gladdens, and this glorious scene inspires and enchants others, *he,* who so loved the beautiful, so delighted in the sun, the sea, the flowers, he is in the cold dark grave, shut out for ever from light, life, and love."

" Oh, Miss Ada !" said old Bessie, " when I heard the poor missus spake them words, although it was to her ain sel' she spake them,—maybe it ill becomes her puir hond-maiden to rebuke the likes o' she,—I culd na keep silence, but I opened my lips and said: 'O missus, dear missus, I never expected to hear the likes o' them words fra your mou'. This a fine grond ootlondish place, na doot, but think you it's to be compared to the New Jerusalem ? Na, na, missus dear ; eye hath na seen, nor ear heard,

neither hath it entered into the heart of man
to conceive, the blessed things He hath prepared for those that love him and do his will;
and who ever loved the Lord or studied mair
to do his will than my dear master? There's
sorrow *here*, missus dear; scarce an English
home where there's na some lovely young
creature fading awa', for a' this fine warm
sun and soft sweet air.   Last night, missus,
I was lying awake thinking over a mony
things, when I heerd a low chaunting sort
o' a noise, and the tramp, tramp, tramp o'
heavy feet, and I got up and looked fra my
window, and there I see a burial procession;
'deed before night was well over I see twa.
The first, the priests and the mourners and
a' were in white; they looked for a' the
warld like so many ghaists; a' held lighted
torches in their honds, and went their way
up the steep street. And I'd scarce got warm
in bed again when I heerd the same chaunt-

ing noise and the same tramping sound, and
this time they were a', priests and followers
and a', in black; that seemed mair like a Christian funeral. But if I wor to die here, missus
dear, I'd na like to be buried at night; it
do seem sa ghastly and unkid. But I mention them burials, missus, to show ye, for a'
the flowers, and the sunshine, and the soft
air o' this place, that where the dear masther
is, is a much better place. There, missus,
sickness and sorrow and pain and death can
never come; there's meetings there, but na
mair partings; tears be wiped fra every face.
Oh, indeed thot's a better lond nor this."

"And what did my mother answer,
Bessie?" I said.

" She put her hond kindly on my shoulder,
Miss Ada, and said, 'You are right, Bessie.
My thoughts, alas! are of the earth, earthy;
they will cling to his dear body in the grave,
they will not rise and try to follow his

blessed spirit to Heaven. Oh, Bessie, when will my lonely pilgrimage be over? when shall I meet my husband, my beloved, again?' I said, ' Oh, missus, dinna be in sich a hum ; think o' poor dear Miss Ada : she's fatherless now, would ye ha' her mitherless also ?' ' Na, na, Bessie,' said my dear missus, drying her eyes. ' Na, its sinfu' in me, a mither, to wish sa and pray sa, to be ta'en out o' this valley o' the shadow o' death. I suld pray to be spared awhile, for the sake of my dear gude dutiful and loving child.' "

What Bessie told me explained to me the fond, and almost apologetic, manner of my darling mother on that our first day at Mentone, and the resolute efforts she made to interest herself in our new home and opening prospects. Alas, the barb was in her heart, even while with Spartan fortitude she hid it and tried to smile.

CHAPTER XV.

VIOLET RIDLEY.

COLONEL RIDLEY and M. de Monleon, accompanied by Violet, the Colonel's daughter, called upon us soon after we had breakfasted, and while we were enjoying from the balcony of our saloon that curious aerial phenomenon of Bordighera separated from the sea by a kind of mirage and suspended as it were in mid air.

Colonel Ridley tried to explain this wondrous optical delusion. He seemed to do so to his own satisfaction, but certainly not to ours; and M. de Monleon, equally puzzled with ourselves, said, " Ah, my dear Colonel, it is like beauty, or love, or genius, or death, a grand mystery; we can think and wonder, and wonder and think, but we can never understand it."

Violet Ridley was a sweet girl, but no one could look at her without a conviction that all her father's hopes and efforts would end in disappointment. Her eyes had that unnatural clearness and brightness, her skin that almost crystal transparency, her cheek that exquisite rose, and her form that painful degree of thinness, which to an experienced eye denote the dread presence of consumption.

Poor Violet! she had no idea of her danger. Her father, who would not believe in it himself, forbade any word that could awaken any suspicion in herself. It was painful to see her so lively, so merry, so full of plans for a future which all felt did not await her on earth. Her cough was very troublesome to her, particularly at night, but she made light of it; and as her appetite and spirits were so good, her father, who loved her with an exclusive fondness, to which she warmly responded, hoped that the soft air of the South would save her yet, and was content to give up his English sports, his club, everything that had been wont to delight him, to winter all his life at Mentone, if by so doing he could save this darling of his heart, his only child.

M. Monleon, like all Mentonese gentle-men of ancient birth, was accomplished, in-tellectual, and eloquent. I never met with a more amiable or better-bred man.

I think he had taken a very great liking to Lady Beatrice, for I noticed that his eyes wandered ever and anon to the door until she had made her appearance, after which he kept them fixed on the carpet, or on Bordighera still apparently suspended in mid air, except when he stole a furtive glance at her fair, aristocratic face.

I had never seen Beatrice in company before, and I was struck with the coldness, reserve, and almost hauteur of her manner to a gentleman who, owing to his kind and timely assistance on the night before, seemed to me to be entitled to the greatest cordiality.

When first Beatrice entered the room she was very pale; but when M. de Monleon rose, and, believing it to be the English custom, warmly extended his hand, the deepest crimson suffused her face; and though she did not actually refuse her hand, yet she gave it in such a manner that he, too, coloured, and felt as if he had committed a breach of etiquette.

He did not offer his hand again in a hurry.

CHAPTER XVI.

THE SWEET SOUTH.

CERTAINLY the soft climate, the cheering sun, and the lively and varied scenery of Mentone, have a wonderful power of raising the spirits and soothing the troubled heart.

At least, as far as I am concerned, I must own that the passionate grief and morbid agony the thought of my father had hitherto caused began to mellow into a soft and not unbearable regret; and that, in the presence of so much that is sublime and grand and exalting in nature, all that concerned that false and, fascinating fortune-hunter, Roscommon Lyall, dwindled into a vanity and a delusion.

His was not a character to flourish in the garden of memory. The greatest charms of person, the softest blandishments of manner, brilliant powers of conversation, grace, style, and even the eloquence of fine dark eyes, and of the smile of a finely-curved mouth, —all irresistible as they certainly are when their possessor is present,—fade away in the memory day by day ; while the recollection of one manly virtue, one heroic deed, one devoted, unselfish act of sublime and con-stant affection flourishes for ever and ever in the memory of the heart, and in absence, wins the fancy away from the sparkling, fas-cinating trifler, to the plain, upright, noble-hearted man who had been completely eclipsed by the brilliant sham.

And thus it was that my mind, elevated

as it was by the grandeur of the scenes among which I now delighted to roam, and looking through nature up to nature's God, I found my thoughts turning with a feeling of shame and self-reproach from the false idol of my young heart, to dwell on the intellectual superiority, the moral rectitude, the fervent gratitude and devoted attachment to my father, of Harry Blake.

Not that for a moment I wished Harry Blake to present himself in the character of an aspirant to my hand. The old Border blood rushed to my brow at the bare thought, which, strange to say, would cross my mind, that he, if he prospered in life, might some day hope to win my love.

No, come what would, I was a Moore of Moordell, and he was Harry Blake, Betty Blake's grandson; but I thought, with Pauline Deschapelles, "If he had but been a poor gentleman!" What then?—he might already have given his heart's first love to another.

" No! no!"   Something within me whispered, " No."

From my earliest girlhood I had felt a sort of conviction—intuitive, instinctive— that Harry Blake loved me,—that I was the hidden Ida of that noble breast, but that while the passionate heart of youth overflowed with love, the consciousness of the difference of our positions,—the sense that I was his benefactor's daughter, — overshadowed that love with feelings of reverence, respect, and even veneration, such as a page might feel for an empress, or a devotee for a saint !

*   *   *   *   *

We took advantage of the glorious weather, which Lucia attributed solely to St. Benoît, to make excursions to the most interesting of the neighbouring ruins and resorts.

Colonel Ridley and Violet, together with M. de Monleon, were always of our party. We used to set out soon after an early breakfast, the ladies on donkeys, the gentlemen walking, and M. de Monleon—who, born a Mentonese, though his mother was a Sardinian, and singularly attached to his native place—enlivened the way by the histories he told us of every river, rock, shrine, and other object of interest.

Very often my dear mother did not accompany us. Her strength had failed her sadly ever since my father's death—that sudden, violent, and terrible death, which had been so awful a shock to the nervous system of his adoring and devoted wife. She preferred to sit by herself, gazing from the drawing-room window at the dark blue sea—thinking, perhaps, as she watched its sapphire ripples, with passionate regret, of the stormier waters of that great Northern Ocean by which she had been wont to wander, during so many happy years, leaning on my dear father's strong and loving arm.

Those waves still surged and moaned round his last resting-place ; and all the beauties of the South were nothing, to my poor mother, compared to that fairy-land which true love had created for her on the bleak sand-hills of Northumberland.

By degrees we became acquainted with many of the English families who were wintering at Mentone. They found us in our mountain rambles, our pic-nics, and our sketching parties ; but visiting, in the ordinary sense of the word, there was none at Mentone.

It was a gentle, hushed, and sympathizing intimacy that existed between families, in

every one of which was at least one consumptive patient.

One, generally "the favourite and the
flower," the most beautiful, beloved, gifted,
and good, had got that "worm in the bud,"
that barb in the young breast, which, in spite
of all that science, and love, and the air of
the sweet South, and devoted care can do,
generally dooms the young victim to an
early grave,—hers all the gain; but, oh!
what endless sorrow—what fever of vain
longing—what a life of morbid regret, perhaps of groundless remorse, for those who
have loved and survived her!—what lasting
misery for the mother, when all besides have
forgotten, or at least have learnt to remember without a pang, that lovely girl,
or that fine, promising man, who died in
the South of France, or at Lisbon, or
Palermo! The mother, in her long despair,
can never forget;—

" ' They weep, but smile at length, and smiling
     weep—
  She never really smiles again.'

To comfort or beguile others, she may force her lips to smile; but that smile which is the heart's sunshine is gone for ever. The shadow of her darling's tomb for ever darkens her path of life !

CHAPTER XVII.

LA BIONDINA.

Violet Ridley and Lady Beatrice were the invalids of our party. Violet's lungs were very seriously affected, and all but her fond, sanguine father could see her daily growing thinner and thinner, more transparent, more painfully beautiful, more spirit-like and unearthly!

Yet she never complained, and though her maid told Proudfoot that she often coughed all through the night, no word of impatience ever passed her lips, and she always spoke cheerily and hopefully of her state.

Lady Beatrice had improved wonderfully since her stay at Mentone. She had gained flesh and colour, strength and spirit. Her cough had greatly diminished, and all fever had left her.

She took a great delight in our excursions and sketching parties. She had a remarkable talent for landscape painting, and, as M. de Monleon was a very accomplished artist, albeit only an amateur, this similarity of tastes and pursuits brought them much together.

Lady Beatrice—who, all gentleness and concession with us, and indeed with all but M. de Monleon—appeared quite an altered character in that gentleman's company. Whether there was anything antagonistic in their natures or not, I cannot tell, and must leave it to those versed in the science of sympathies to decide; but the pale, mild, acquiescent girl became, at his approach, haughty, brilliant, and almost saucy in her airs and repartees. A war of words, an encounter of wits, a clash of the small swords of argument, was always going on between them. In spite of this, it was evident to me that he admired Lady Beatrice enthusiastically. His eyes followed her wherever she went. He never forgot a word she said, an opinion she expressed, a wish that escaped her. Frequently he risked his life to get her a flower on some precipice, if he saw her blue eye fixed on it.

She was exactly the sort of girl to awaken the deepest, most ardent passion in the enthusiastic, poetical, fervent nature of a son of the South. Fair, with a fairness of which even in the north. there are few specimens, and which, perhaps, was partly owing to her extreme delicacy of constitution; of almost crystal transparency, yet with a roseate bloom; dark and very large violet eyes,

with long black lashes, and soft brown eye-
brows ; a profusion of silky hair, of a delicate
blonde hue, with a golden gloss on its rich
folds ; a very long throat ; tall and very
slender form, and limbs of perfect beauty :
such was Lady Beatrice, whose perfect features were rather German than Roman, but
had nothing of the stony, unintellectual cast
of the former. Her beautiful lips were of
the red of the mountain-ash berries, and her
teeth were of that pearly brilliancy and
beauty which so often belong to those in
whom consumption is inherent. M. de Monleon offered to give Lady Beatrice some instruction in landscape painting. She said
that when she felt she required instruction
she would apply to him ; but she said it with
such a toss of her pretty little head that he
laughed, and replied—

" Perhaps you consider yourself better
adapted to be my rival than my pupil ? "

"Perhaps I do," she replied; but in spite of this rebuff, Alphonse de Monleon, finding one day some sketches of Lady Beatrice's on the drawing-room table, corrected some little faults in perspective, threw in a few masterly figures and a tree or two, and had just begun to wash in the sea and sky, when Lady Beatrice came in and snatched her sketch-book away. She tried to frown and look very angry, but she burst into a fit of laughter in spite of herself, and acknowledged how much her drawings had gained from the master's touch. I saw the tears in Alphonse de Monleon's fine dark eyes as Beatrice said these, the only kind words she had ever addressed to him. I felt certain from that moment that he loved her. I was confirmed in this opinion some time after. Beatrice, in her wilful habit of never doing anything Alphonse de Monleon advised, and doing everything he warned her against, had left

the sunny for the shady side of the street,
when we were all walking out together.
She laughed in playful defiance as she did so,
at the pale and terrified Alphonse, who, re-
gardless of etiquette and of the distance at
which Lady Beatrice always kept him, rushed
across the street, and, taking her hand, compelled her to come back to the sunny side of
the way. But the evil was done. From
the sun to the shade at Mentone is like the
suddenly passing from July to January,
from the torrid to the frigid zone; and
this is why so many consumptive patients
get rapidly worse in this beautiful spot.
It is the nature of the disease to make
them rash and sanguine. Beatrice paid
dearly for this pleasure of tormenting Alphonse de Monleon. The next day she
was very ill in bed. Poor Alphonse called
several times during the day to inquire how
Lady Beatrice was. Lucia told me, with

tears of sympathy in her fine dark eyes, that
M. de Leon look like " one miserable : " she
had picked up a few English words in our
service, and in that of another English family
she had served.

" Oh, Signorina," said Lucia, laying her
hand on her heart; "il povero Monsieur de
Monleon, he love la superba biondina; if
she die, he no live long. Amor ! amor ! oh,
it is a pain !"

" Do you say that ' from experience,
Lucia ?" I asked in Italian.

Lucia blushed and sighed, and that was
sufficient reply.

We were all very anxious about Lady
Beatrice, and were constantly in her room.
Dr. B—— was with us, and did all that
science and devoted attention could do for
the beautiful sufferer, who, in spite of her
burning fever, her galloping pulse, her difficulty of breathing, and her tormenting cough,

was in excellent spirits, and would not own
that she felt very ill. But after the doctor
left us, the wilful girl insisted on getting up;
and throwing on her wrapper, she, before
any one knew what she meant to do, hurried
to the window of her room. Perhaps in her
secret heart she knew that M. de Monleon
loved her, and she felt certain that, if so, he
must be watching for Dr. B——, to waylay
him as he left our house. If so, she was
right. It was mid-day, and, despite the
burning sun, M. de Monleon stood watching
for Dr. B——. Poor Alphonse! he looked
like the ghost of his former self; and when,
in reply to his eager inquiries, Dr. B——
shook his head, had not the doctor thrown
his arm around him, he would have fallen
senseless to the ground.

I had followed Beatrice to the window,
fearing some draught of air, and I tried to
draw her away. The doctor had led M.

de Monleon into the house of a Mentonese nobleman who lived close by.

"Poor Alphonse!" murmured Beatrice, as she suffered me to draw her away from the window, and yielded to my entreaties that she would return to bed. A very severe attack of pleurisy, one of the prevailing maladies of the Mentonese, followed this act of imprudence, and Lady Beatrice did not leave her room for a fortnight from this time. When, at length, Dr. B——'s judicious care and wondrous skill brought her safely through this dangerous attack, and looking like some beautiful spirit—so pure, so transparent, and so fragile—in her pale blue satin wrapper, trimmed with swan's-down, and a lace *fichu* covering her pretty little head and splendid blonde tresses, she received M. de Monleon in our salon. The strong man trembled; his cheek had the ashen hue of death; and when he marked the change her late illness had wrought in her already fragile form, he suddenly turned away, and, burying his face in his handkerchief, sobbed like a child or a woman.

The weather, which during Lady Beatrice's illness had been frequently wet and cold, was now as fine and warm as an ordinary June in England; and she was all anxiety, after her long confinement, to resume our donkey rides and sketching parties. As Dr. B—— did not object, stipulating only that we should avoid the shade, and never be out after sunset—a rule he strictly enforced with all his patients—it was agreed that we should make excursions to Bordighera, Castellace, Rocca Bruna, Dolceaqua, Ventimiglia, Gerbeo, and St. Agnese. For the particulars of these delightful excursions, and, indeed, of our winter at Mentone, I shall now have recourse to the journal I kept while in that enchanted spot.

MY JOURNAL.

EXTRACTS FROM THE JOURNAL KEPT
BY ME, ADA MOORE, DURING THE
WINTER OF 186—, AT MENTONE.

CHAPTER XVIII.

A VISIT TO CASTELLACE.

January 10.—The weather was so exquisitely fine, the sun so bright, and the air so balmy, that we gladly agreed to a proposal made by Colonel Ridley and M. de Monleon, who called while we were sitting at breakfast with our windows open, that we should avail ourselves of this glorious day to pay a long projected visit to Castellace. Lady Beatrice, though still looking dangerously delicate and transparently beautiful, declared that she felt quite equal to the excursion.

M. de Monleon and herself had resumed
their half-playful warfare. He never knew
that she had seen him from the windows of
her room when he all but fainted at hearing Dr. B——'s serious view of her case.
He was much too dignified and intellectual a
man to play the sorry part of a despairing
lover.

That he was passionately attached to Lady
Beatrice I had no doubt, because I had witnessed his anguish when she was in danger;
but he wisely avoided all marked attentions
to the haughty and capricious beauty, and
often forced himself to appear to prefer the
society of Violet Ridley or myself.

On this day my mother, who was more
than usually pale, could not be induced to
join our party. Poor dear mother! when
she came down to breakfast I could see by
her eye-lids, which were red and swollen,
that she had been weeping; but she forced

herself to smile, and to appear to take an interest in our intended excursion, in order not to damp our spirits.

When we had taken leave of her, and indeed had set out, I found I had left my sketch-book behind. I hurried upstairs, and was entering the sitting-room, when I saw my dear mother's graceful form kneeling by the couch, and in her hand she held my poor father's picture, on the glass of which her tears were falling like rain.

I took my sketch-book noiselessly from a little table close to the door, and quietly retraced my steps. On the stairs I met Bessie.

" Bessie," I said, " my dear Mamma seems very low to-day. I am obliged to go on this excursion, but I depend on you to try all you can to cheer and comfort my dear mother. Don't let her be long alone. She seems more dejected than usual to-day."

" Eh, Sirs !" said Bessie, " and wha can marvel at that, seeing this is her wedding-day, poor dear ! Oh, the glodsome onnivarsary it was wont to be at Muredell. Ilka year they twa becam mair truly ain flesh and ain speerit. Wha con morvel the lane widow is weel-nigh broken-hearted the day ?"

" Perhaps I had better stay with her, Bessie," I said.

" Na, na ! ye'll maybe fash her. Let her be ; let her be. She is na ain to sorrow like they that ha' na hope, but she's best by her sel' this sod and solemn onnivarsary."

I thought Bessie was perhaps right ; and again begging her to attend to my dear mother, I joined my party ; but my heart felt very heavy, and I blamed myself for having forgotten that this was a day which, as far back as I could remember, had been an annual holiday and festival at Moordell Vicarage.

It was a day on which, in our childhood, Harry Blake and I had had no lessons to learn,—on which all the married couples in the little village were invited to tea and supper in the Vicarage kitchen,—on which my dear mother always gave my father some little present, at which she had worked in secret, and on which he presented her with some little ornament purchased on the sly.

On this day my father always made a bowl of punch, and Bessie a noble cake; and Harry Blake, in spite of the season, contrived to bring a bouquet from the flower-pots on his grandmother's window-sill, and made a speech to my mother in Latin, composed by my father; and I had forgotten that this was that day of days, the wedding day of those beloved parents.

Oh, volatile, forgetful youth! And yet I dearly loved my father, and I had truly mourned him; nay, I have never ceased to

love and to mourn him ; but in very early
youth new scenes and new impressions have
a power for a time to fill the mind so as to
exclude the past, not permanently, but at
least till the deep wound is skinned over.

At my mother's age it is not so. New
scenes and new faces had no power to di-
rect her mind from the one absorbing memory, the one solitary image for ever en-
shrined in her heart—the lover of her youth,
the husband of her choice, the partner of
her life, and the idol of her constant affections.

All day long, in spite of the glorious sunshine, the balmy air, and the enchanting
scenery, my mind and heart were ever and
anon darkened by two shadows.

First, that of my dear mother's form in
her widow's garb, as she knelt by the couch
with my father's picture in her hand ; and
the tomb of that dear kind father, as I had

so often knelt and wept beside it beneath the dark yew-tree in Moordell Church.

As we passed the Hôtel des Quatre Nations, and, mounted on our donkeys, took the little path, bordered by two walls and overhung with oranges, which diverges from our street, Lady Beatrice's donkey stumbled.

In a moment, M. de Monleon was by her side.

I noticed that he was pale, and trembling with alarm, for Beatrice was very nearly thrown; but, in return for his anxiety, she laughed saucily, and refused his proffered aid. I saw he was wounded, and I was glad that he had the spirit promptly to revenge himself.

And thus it happened : when we came to the base of the yellow tufa rocks behind Mentone, and were proceeding along the donkey path to the high terraces covered with olives, that look down even on the loftiest heights of Mentone, my donkey and Lady Beatrice's were seized with fits of obstinacy, not uncommon to the asinine of all kinds. They even showed a disposition to lie down in the dirty winding path.

We had only two drivers, one of whom was far in advance, attending to Violet Ridley's donkey; the other had dropped his stick on the road, and was gone back to look for it. Missing, then, not only the " *Ulla !* " (meaning " Allez !") and the " *Isa !*" ("Shame !") of the driver, but that much stronger argument the stick, " Biondina " and " Brunetta "—my light grey and Lady Beatrice's dark brown donkey—resolved to have their own way, and lie down.

Vainly Beatrice tried to urge her donkey on. Colonel Ridley and Violet were a good way in advance, he walking by Violet's side as M. de Monleon was by ours.

M. de Monleon, not appearing to take the slightest notice of Beatrice's situation, exerted himself to keep my donkey up, and to get him on. In this he succeeded, and I was fast overtaking Violet and her father, when a loud scream from Lady Beatrice made us look round.

The high-born damsel and her donkey were both lying in the dust, and there seemed some danger of the donkey's rolling over the prostrate lady.

M. de Monleon, seeing this, and hearing Lady Beatrice call him by name and implore his assistance, rushed back to her.

I followed on my donkey, who went willingly enough in that direction, for it was that of his home. I reached the spot in time to see Lady Beatrice lifted by Alphonse out of the dust and on to her donkey, and to hear M. de Monleon say to her—

" Pride shall have a fall, miladi !"

Lady Beatrice blushed, bit her lip, and turned away her head to hide the tears that rose to her eyes. The next moment she held out her hand to Alphonse de Monleon, and said, in Italian, "Forgive me, and do not desert me!" in a manner so bewitching that I am certain he felt disposed to fall at her feet or to clasp her to his heart.

As I gazed at that delicate, blonde, Northern beauty, and that dark, handsome, and most interesting Mentonese nobleman, as they moved on among the pine woods in view of the magnificent mountain range of St. Agnese, the blue sea in the distance, and heath and myrtle springing up beside us, I thought how much the ephemeral beauty of those two human beings added to the interest of that scene, whose grandeur and sublimity had lasted for thousands of years, and probably will endure for thousands of years to come.

M. de Monleon, who was in very high
spirits after his reconciliation with Lady
Beatrice, told us many anecdotes of the
banditti-like behaviour of the peasants of
Castellace at the close of the last century,
when they rivalled the bravoes of Venice
and the brigands of Naples in cruelty, theft,
and daring.

Many noble *émigrés* of both sexes, who
had escaped the guillotine and the red
ruffianism of the Reign of Terror, were
robbed and murdered in the unfrequented
paths and craggy passes of the mountains
of St. Agnese, while trying to escape into
Sardinia, and yet the descendants of these
bandits are among the gentlest and most
good-humoured of peasants.

They never pass a stranger without a
friendly greeting; and if they approach, it
is not to attack, to rob, or assault, but to
offer a service, or to utter a " God speed !"

Long before we reached Castellace, we could see the roofs of its quaint old houses, and the tower of its church, rising above the groves of olive-trees.

The town is composed of three little streets, and even Cologne · itself is not half so offensive to the olfactory nerves as this picturesque and quaint old Castellace.

Mentone, not the most fragrant place in the world, and by some considered disagreeable to a delicate nostril, is a pattern of cleanliness compared to Castellace ; and yet, in spite of its dirt and its effluvia, there is something to an artist's eye irresistibly captivating in Castellace ; and, as we were all provided with sketch-books and eager to begin, we agreed that there were such an abundance of promising Prout-like bits, that *l'embarras de richesses* made it difficult on what to fix. I resolved to enrich my sketch-book with the view of the church, with its tall red tower.

Lady Beatrice was bent on sketching the antique residence of the Lascaris, a family of historic renown. To reach this abode she had to descend from her donkey's back, and make her way, on foot, through a very narrow archway.

Warned by past experience, M. de Monleon did not offer to accompany her; and perceiving that he was settling himself down to sketch a quaint old house and some very ragged, dirty, picturesque groups, who were attracted by our party, she smiled and said, "M. de Monleon, an unprotected female wants your help and advice. Do come and fix my point of sight, and my horizontal line, my middle distance, and my foreground!"

Joy sparkled in Alphonse de Monleon's fine dark eyes, as he yielded to Lady Beatrice's playful entreaty, and followed her through the narrow archway into the little piazza where the house of the Lascaris stood. What stagnation, as far as industry goes, appears to reign in all these quaint old towns! The *dolce far niente* seems to be universal; no one in Castellace seemed to have any business to attend to, any work to do, any duty to perform. It seemed to me that the whole town turned out to stare at us.

All the ordinary occupations that keep English housewives so busy are at a standstill in Castellace. There is no washing, drying, starching, or ironing, for the whole population are unwashed.

There is no mending, making, patching, darning, for rags, picturesque, many-coloured and fluttering in the soft sunny breeze, are the *grande mode* at Castellace.

There were no symptoms of cooking, no smoke issuing from the chimney. The babies seemed to bring themselves up, or to nurse each other; and every one seemed merry and happy. I suppose that like their long-legged, attenuated sheep, they feed on the lemons that grow within their reach; but, soberly speaking, a chestnut soup and a little maccaroni is all they require.

What a contrast to our poor! In our climate, who can live without fire? People must work hard to get the necessaries of life. Idleness in England is starvation. In Castellace people do not starve, even if they will not work. They have, however, one immense advantage over the English poor,— they have no bottle-imp to bewitch them, no evil spirit to tempt them, no gin-palaces where they can barter body and soul for 'blue ruin' or 'Old Tom.'

I entered into conversation with some of the ragged idlers who crowded round me to watch and comment on the progress of my sketch. I had learnt from Lucia a good deal of the Mentonese patois, but in every village the dialect varies; still I contrived to make them understand me; and when I asked them how they liked the annexation to France, they shook their heads, and their eyes flashed, and one man began an anathema on the change and on the taxes, when the others nudged him and gave him to understand that I might be a spy, after which. he became sullen and silent. Still, wherever I go, and from all I can learn from Lucia and old Marta, our other native servant, the the people are terribly disappointed in the result of the annexation, which they asked for principally in the hope that it would facilitate their trade in lemons, whereas in reality the effect has been the very reverse.

After we had finished our sketches, and partaken of some refreshments which we had brought with us, and which we spread on a terrace beneath the olives close to Castellace, we resolved to lionize the quaint old

town, and then to return to Mentone. It
would not be safe, as we well knew, for
either Lady Beatrice or Violet Ridley to be
out after sunset.

The spot we had chosen for our banqueting
hall was one sheet of brilliant and varie-
gated blossoms. The golden narcissus, the
purple anemone, and some brilliant scarlet
pink and blue flowers new to me, for I had
never seen them in any other country, bloomed
as freely, perfectly wild, at Castellace, in
January, as our garden flowers do in June
under the care of skilful gardeners.

Lady Beatrice and M. de Monleon were
very good friends on this occasion. His
sketch of the house of the Lascaris, drawn
as he had advised and directed, was singularly spirited and effective ; and on the whole,
what with the glorious weather, the sublime
prospect, the exhilarating mountain breeze,
the beauty and fragrance of the flowers, and

the verdure of the feathery olives that sheltered us, it was a most enjoyable excursion
to all save myself.   I, in the midst of all
sunshine and beauty, could not but see, in
my mind's eye, my poor father's tomb by
the great German Ocean, and my mother's
dark-robed form kneeling by the couch, and
the tear-blurred glass of his miniature in her
thin white hand.

Yes ! when I remembered that this day
of sunshine and bloom here, was that same
14th of January on which *they* had been
wedded, all the beauty and brightness died
away, and I could not suppress my tears.

From the terrace where we were pic-nic-
ing, we had a delightful view of two ancient
chapels, dedicated to St. Antonio and St.
Sebastiano.

M. de Monleon, who was a first-rate
archæologist, informed us that St. Sebastiano
was a Romanesque building of great an-

tiquity ; and Colonel Ridley, who was also
an antiquarian, and M. de Monleon, went
into ecstasies, while contemplating its round
apse.

While lionizing the little town, we looked
in at the grated windows of several old di-
lapidated chapels. They belonged to different orders of monks, but all were equally
dusty, dirty, and neglected. In all, we
could see tinsel and artificial flowers, gilded
lanterns, and ragged, faded banners, which
are never used but in honour of the patron
saint of the chapel, and in the annual procession in his honour.

In returning we took the route from the
chapel of St. Sebastiano, through the valley
that opens into the Mentonese churchyard.
Colonel Ridley and M. de Monleon were in
a fever of anxiety lest we should not get
b ack before sunset, for the path through this
valley is so winding, that it seemed nearly

to double the length of our journey. However, La Biondina and La Brunetta, who knew they were going home, trotted along with such goodwill, that before the dreaded and sudden change from summer heat to winter cold had come, we had reached home in safety.

" Guess wha's come, Miss Ada," said Bessie, coming out to help me off my donkey, and her honest old face radiant with joy.

"Any one from England, Bessie?" I said, my heart beating, I know not why.

" Twa fra the Border, Miss, — Harry Blake that wor—Master Blake that is—and Mr. Fenwick o' Fenwick, mair blind nor a bot !"

I rushed upstairs to the salon. There was Harry Blake, sitting by my mother's side ; and, in an arm-chair opposite, I beheld the colossal form, and stern, handsome face of Fenwick of Fenwick. My dear mother seemed cheered by this unexpected visit from those who had so loved her husband. Both knew it was her wedding day—that day which had always been such a white day at Moordell Vicarage, and they had managed to arrive on this day to comfort and cheer her.

Soon after our departure Bessie had rushed up to tell my mother that Harry Blake and Fenwick o' Fenwick were in the hall below.

It seemed that one day Fenwick of Fenwick, calling on our dear old French Count, met Harry Blake there. Mr. Fenwick's blindness had increased so much, that he could not distinguish Harry Blake's features, but he took a fancy to his voice, his manners, and his refined and sensible conversation. Fenwick of Fenwick was looking out for some young man, at once a scholar and a gentleman, to travel with him, after having

first passed some weeks with him at Fenwick
Park, to arrange the valuable works in his
fine old library, and to take a catalogue of
them. But Harry Blake had very good
prospects at Oxford,—pupils during term
and during the long vacation. When Mr.
Fenwick met him at the Count's, he was
taking a holiday to recruit his health, which
had been shaken by my dear father's sudden
and dreadful death. Harry did not at first
consent to travel with Mr. Fenwick, but he
consented to go with him to Fenwick Park,
and readily agreed to arrange his library
and take a catalogue of his books. It was
an occupation after Harry's own heart—he
was an epicure in books.

Mr. Fenwick had been a book-collector all
his life. His great wealth had enabled him
to gratify this very expensive taste. Poor
fellow, he doated on every rare old black-
letter volume still, although he could scarcely

distinguish the quaint old cover and the silver clasps.

I heard all these particulars from Harry Blake himself. He told me that he became so fascinated with his employment, and Mr. Fenwick and he grew so partial to each other, that he was scarcely aware of the flight of time,—so pleasantly the days passed in the company of those silent friends the books, and so genial and cheerful were the evenings in Mr. Fenwick's company. Harry Blake told me that one evening, the conversation happening to fall on Harry's early life and education, he was speaking with enthusiastic gratitude of his benefactor and tutor (my dear father), when, to his surprise, he saw the tears stealing from Mr. Fenwick's blind eyes down his now sallow and furrowed cheeks. Mr. Fenwick explained to him that the Vicar of Moordell had been his best and dearest friend; and from that time, Harry

said, my father, my mother, and myself
were their frequent theme. Nor were we
talked of less frequently or less enthusiastically when Mr. Fenwick invited the
old French Count and the Italian Signore,—
those dear, dear friends of my childhood,
to spend some time with him at Fenwick
Park.

The Signore was, Harry said, in a state of
great excitement. The true patriots of Italy,
after so many disappointments and such a
long heart-sickness arising from hope de-
ferred, had endured and striven on until
the dark clouds of despair began to disperse,
and the day-star of Liberty to dawn in the
South. The name of GARIBALDI was written
in every true Italian heart ; and though only
whispered in secret as yet, all felt it would,
ere long, be proudly proclaimed by every
Italian lip.

" As I listened to the Signore," said Harry,

" the dear Signore who had been so kind to me in my boyhood, and from whom I had learnt the sweet language of the South, I felt the glow of his heart communicate itself to mine. I longed to be a soldier, that I might help in the glorious work of the regeneration of Italy. The Signore, who was about himself to join Garibaldi, would gladly have taken me with him as a volunteer. I would have absented myself from Oxford for a time, to lend a helping hand to the sublime work then going on in Italy, but just at this time Mr. Fenwick was taken very ill. He had become accustomed to me and to my presence, and he implored me not to leave him. I had not the heart to refuse him. Harsh and stern as he seems to others, to me he had been all gentleness. He had wound himself round my heart. I saw him alone in the world, ill, blind (or very nearly so), desolate, and unhappy—at the thought of parting with me,—and so I agreed to remain with him. His doctor advised his spending the winter in Italy or the south of France, and one day he proposed to me to accompany him to Mentone. I have heard, he said, smiling archly, that the widow and daughter of my late dear old friend, the Vicar of Moordell, are passing the winter at Mentone. 'Now,' said he, 'Mentone is the very place my physician recommended for my winter quarters; and if you, my dear young friend, will take charge of a poor purblind valetudinarian on the journey, and stay with him there, I will quadruple whatever you would have made by pupils at Oxford during the same time.' The offer was too tempting for me to refuse it," said Harry Blake, blushing deeply as he added, "Wherever the widow and child of my benefactor are, there my heart is! Besides, I think the dear old Signore, whose mother was a Mentonese of high birth, will contrive to pay us a visit here; and then, if I can leave Mr. Fenwick in your care and strike a blow in the noble cause of Italia Bella and Garibaldi the Brave, I should feel as if I had done something to enrich the peasant blood and gild the humble name of Harry Blake!"

"But you might be wounded, Harry," I said; "you might be killed."

"So much the better," he cried. "In such a cause, were I to die a martyr hero, you might shed a tear over my grave. And what have I to live for?"

"For shame, Harry!" I said. "At your age and with your prospects, you have no excuse for such despondency and discontent. Why, you have never known a sorrow, Harry."

"Wise judges are we of each other!" he replied. "I have known nothing else; my life has been one feverish longing after the unattainable — one long despair—the sighing of the moth for the star."

I did not appear to understand him, but in my inmost heart I pitied him, and felt a strange wish to comfort him. He was such a noble-hearted, intellectual young man, with so fine a form, so beautiful a counte- nance, such a gentlemanly bearing, and such generous impulses. He looked, too, so very unhappy. There were tears in his fine eyes, and the pallor of despair on his cheek.

"Still," I said to myself, " I am a Moore of Moordell; the oldest and noblest blood of the Borderland flows in my veins. He is Harry Blake, the peasant born,—Betty Blake's grandson. I dare not trust myself to pity him, for I know that pity is akin to love, and I remember the old saying, 'When we learn to pity, how soon we learn to love!' It would, I thought, be so disgraceful to a daughter of my house to love a low-born man—a grandson of Betty Blake !

CHAPTER XIX.

NEWS FROM MOORDELL.

January 15*th.*—My dear mother has invited
Mr. Fenwick and Harry Blake to come to
breakfast. They are staying at the Hôtel
des Quatre Nations, but they prefer our
déjeûner à l'Anglaise, with the grand tea
Mr. Willoughby supplies us with, and rolls
baked by Bessie, and buttered toast when
we can get butter, to anything the hotel can
offer. N.B.—My beloved mother has looked
a shade less pale and a little more animated
since the arrival of our friends. How lovely

she still is! Her features are like finely-chiselled ivory, and that *memento mori*, the widow's cap, so unbecoming to coarse features, red faces, and high check-bones, seems to me to show off to advantage the delicate beauty of her lineaments, and the transparency of her lily-white complexion. She takes an interest in all the Moordell news. Mr. Fenwick tells us that the ex-Begum Lady Moore and her son Selim are living very "*fast*," and spending their money lavishly; that all the mothers and daughters in the neighbourhood are trying to ensnare Sir Selim, but that he has declared he will yet win the hand and heart of his cousin Ada Moore, or live and die a bachelor.

"I think he is on the high-road to ruin," said Mr. Fenwick, "for he plays high, has horses on the turf, and it is said that he drinks hard too. Lady Moore is also sus-

pected of a great though secret devotion to
rum and whisky, and I hear that the redness
of her face, and the extreme irritability of
her temper, confirm this report. However,
she still keeps up some of her Eastern customs, and only shows that now red and
bloated face to lady visitors. Her form is
said to have become enormously obese, and
perfectly shapeless. Mr. Fenwick told us,
also, that he had heard that old Hodgson
was on the eve of bankruptcy; that Roscommon Lyall and his wife did not live happily
together; and that young Hodgson was in
the Insolvent Debtors' Court, in company
with Roscommon Lyall. The new Vicar of
Moordell, he said, was a good, steady, pious
young man, and his wife was a well-meaning
woman; but the former was a cold, uninter-
esting preacher, intolerable to those who
had so delighted in my dear father's fervid
eloquence, warm from the heart; while the

tactless interference and cold meddling of Mrs. Lefevre in the cottages of the poor, was always contrasted with the delicate attentions of my dear mother, and the comparison was very unfavourable to the Lefevres.

CHAPTER XX.

ROCCABRUNA.

As the weather, on this the 15th of January, was exquisite, it was proposed that we should make an excursion to Roccabruna.

My mother declined being of the party, and Mr. Fenwick was too blind to enjoy the scenery. I expected that he would have been willing to stay at home with her, but he was resolved to be of the party.

With his stick and his man-servant he accompanied us, leaning on Harry's arm and appearing to enjoy the brightness and beauty of the atmosphere, and to inhale with rapture the varied odour of the flowers, although he could scarcely see more than the difference between light and darkness.

I do not know whether Mr. Fenwick had any suspicion that his new favourite and *protégé*, Harry Blake, was attached to me; but he certainly took every opportunity of praising him in my presence, and of expatiating on all he meant to do for him.

It was a great relief to me to find that Mr. Fenwick had resigned all lover-like pretensions himself, and had assumed a fatherly manner in his conduct towards me. If I had not known Harry Blake to be so very shy, so timid, and so sensitive, I should have imagined that he had made Mr. Fenwick his confidant.

It was a curious fact that although Mr. Fenwick certainly *was* very nearly blind, and that his numerous accidents, mistakes, and blunders betrayed his infirmity, he always talked and acted as if he were in possession of that greatest of blessings, good sight.

I have since noticed this rather affecting peculiarity in other blind people; but, at the time of which I write, I knew no other person suffering from this dreadful affliction.

Mr. Fenwick had brought with him to Mentone a young fellow, who, from his boyhood (indeed ever since his master's sight had been impaired), had been in the habit of walking by his side, acting as an 'eye' to the blind, and describing to him the scenes through which they were passing, and those in the distance.

In Northumberland this lad was always called "the squire's eye" and "second sight;" and by his help Mr. Fenwick was able to keep up, as he believed, the impres-

sion that he beheld the objects around him,
and the prospect in perspective.

"Jock," the youth in question, was a
ruddy, red-haired, good-tempered Border
lad, with a very broad accent and a very
decided burr. He was about twenty, and
was devotedly attached to his master, who,
haughty and stern to his other servants, was
very kind, indulgent, and affable to Jock.

Jock's services were very liberally remu-
nerated. It was only fair that they should
have been so, for Jock was more essential to
Mr. Fenwick's comfort than any other servant in his large and well-appointed establishment.

Mr. Fenwick had all his life been a great
walker. When his impaired sight made
reading and writing impossible, and indoor
life in consequence unbearable, he walked a
good deal further and faster than before,
and Jock had, when quite a little fellow, to

keep pace with the strides of a master of six feet four.

However, the exercise had done Jock no harm. He had grown up from a short, clumsy, freckled boy, into a tall, smart, good-looking young fellow; and many a dark eye followed Jock with interest, but none seemed to awaken a reciprocal feeling save that of my merry Abigail, Lucia.

When I saw poor Jock redden to the roots of his carroty hair if Lucia appeared, and beheld him ever on the alert to help her in any domestic work she had in hand; and when Bessie told me that " tha' young fule o' a Jock was spending gude siller in gewgaws and gimcrocks for Lucy, which the lossie," added Bessie, " wha has a joe o' her ain, is discreet eno' to decline," I spoke to Lucia on the subject.

I remember when I did so it was night, and we were standing by my open window,

from which one could see several small habi-
tations and orange-gardens belonging to the
poor.

"Lucia," I said, "I hope you do not
trifle with the affections of poor Jock."

Lucia blushed, and said, "No, Signorina;
I know too well what love is, to trifle with
so serious a passion. I like Jock; he is a
good-tempered, kind, ready lad, but my love
is already plighted. Look there, Signorina
cara. Do you see yon light?—that light
belongs to Francesco, my intended. We
have been engaged from the time I was
fifteen and he seventeen, that is three years
ago. But we are not like some silly lovers
here, who marry before they have a house
to live in, or an orange-garden to support
them. Still we are both saving money.
We have a house in view, and we have
already bought that piece of ground where
you see that light twinkling, and Francesco

often works there for hours at night, although he must be very tired, poor fellow, for he is a journeyman carpenter, and has a hard taskmaster."

" And when do you expect to be rich enough to marry, Lucia?" I asked.

" If we go on steadily for another year and a half," said Lucia, " we shall be able to make up the 500 francs the house near the cemetery costs. We have 300 francs towards it, and next year the orange and lemon trees Francesco has planted will yield fruit—his first harvest. Fancy, Signorina, that garden where he is now working, and where the orange and lemon trees are so flourishing, was a barren rock less than three years ago. Poor Francesco for my sake has carried up that steep every shovelful of earth in which the trees are planted.

" The first year, during his leisure hours— and he has none but at night—he carried up the earth, prepared the soil, and planted the wild trees. The next year he grafted them, and soon he will begin to gather the fruit.

" Oh, it has been heavy labour; but he says is a labour of love, and that he would much rather take me to a snug home and an orange-garden, than marry like Renzo, his cousin, on nothing, and then have to struggle on to get a house and an orange garden.

" Poor Maria, who was silly enough to marry Renzo, used to work with him at night in their orange-garden, but she caught a cold, which flew to her chest, and she died. This was a lesson to Francesco; when he followed Maria to the cemetery, he vowed no wife of his should work in the cold, dark hours to make an orange-garden. But I wish we had enough to buy the house, said Lucia, sighing and blushing; " for Francesco is wearing himself out with the orange-garden, and is so lonely, and looks so ill.

Oh, Signorina, never fear my giving any encouragement to 'Monsieur Jock,' or any other young man ; I would not be so false and so ungrateful to my own true love, who deprives himself of sleep, and, from his looks, I much fear of food too, to have a comfortable home and an income for his bride."

This little narrative interested me much, and I often from my window watched with lively interest that "light of love," poor Francesco's lantern, as it flitted to and fro during the dark hours which he spent in watering and tending his orange-garden.

I told the simple tale to Bessie, who said nothing at the time, but "They say, Miss Ada, luve will still be lord of a'. I'm thankfu' to say I'm an exception to that rule, Miss Ada. I never wor in luve, and I hope I never may be sican a fule."

"Who can tell, Bessie ?" I replied. "They say there's no fool like an old fool !"

" 'Deed then, Miss, you're right there," said Bessie; " for if you'll believe it, Proudfute is making hersel' downright ridiculous aboot a jaunty flaunty chop o' a courier over the way. The stuck-up auld, fule tells ilka ain thot she's a tidy bit o' siller laid by, and I believe Laird Tounley's courier ha' got an inkling o' the same; for there's sican a complimenting, and booing, and scraping, and grinning, ganging on atween him ond Proudfute, mortal mon never see the like, and she auld eno' to be the roystering lad's mither !' "

Bessie was not only very proud of never having been in love, but she had no patience with any fellow-servant of hers who was more susceptible than herself; and if the victim of the Boy God happened to be " uppish in years," as Bessie called it, the old Borderer's contempt and disgust were withering indeed.

But to return to this June-like 15th of January.

When breakfast was over Mr. Fenwick proposed an excursion; and after some debate as to which beautiful spot in this neighbourhood, so rich in objects of historic, romantic, and picturesque interest, should be selected for this day's enjoyment, Ventimiglia and Bordighera were fixed upon.

CHAPTER XXI.

VENTIMIGLIA.

At Mr. Fenwick's entreaty, my dear mother agreed to be of the party. She had been rather less absorbed and depressed since the arrival of Mr. Fenwick and Harry Blake. I began, therefore, to hope that her first wild burst of anguish had at length wept itself away, and that, as "all suffering doth destroy or is destroyed even by the sufferer," so my darling mother's grief had taken that turn which grief must take, unless it is to wear out the heart that nurses it.

Alas! I little guessed what it was, con-
nected with Mr. Fenwick's stay at Mentone,
that had restored some degree of peace to
my dear mother's pale face, and rekindled
in her soft eyes a ray of contentment.   But
of this hereafter.

Mr. Fenwick had proposed to my mother
that while the young and enterprising of the
party, armed with their sketch-books, should
perform the journey as usual,—the gentle-
men on foot and the ladies on donkeys,—
she should accompany him in a comfortable
open vetturino.   It is a beautiful drive of
about five miles, from Mentone to Ventimiglia, along the Genoa Cornice.   The
whole party on this bright day set out in
good humour.   The two invalids, Violet and
Beatrice, were looking better than usual;
and when we reached the village of St.
Mauro, Lady Beatrice insisted on M. de
Monleon's helping her to take a sketch of

the little painted church on the olive-
covered promontory that contrasts so beautifully with the exquisite blue of the sea.

After we had—at least all the artists of
the party—taken a sketch of the church,
and after the driver of the vetturino had
passed the custom-house with the ordinary
assurance that the parties he was driving
were taking an airing only, not a "voyage,"
we proceeded along the picturesque road,
and that great fortress, the Castle of Ventimiglia, rose in all its majesty and beauty
before us, its white walls contrasting finely
with the brown precipice on which it stands.
All the sketch-books were immediately in
requisition.

Lady Beatrice, who had formerly been so
opinionated and independent, now always
asked and took Alphonse de Monleon's advice, and even submitted to his throwing in
a few bold strokes,—a masterly tree, a cow,

a goat, a few sheep, or a spirited group of figures.

Nothing could be more animated or pictu-resque than the appearance of Ventimiglia. The town is built on a ledge of rocks skirt-ing the sea; and much that is antique and venerable, in the shape of deserted convents and quaint old houses, grey or brown with time, is thrown into strong relief by the many-coloured towers of the brightest hues that abound here. All this is on the rocky height, while far below nestles a little port to which fishing-smacks and some curious pointed rocks gave animation.

The Grande Rue of Ventimiglia, like all the streets of their quaint old towns, is very narrow. The houses on either side speak of former grandeur; many of them are curiously painted on the outside with figures of ani-mals, others are adorned with marble bal-conies,—an evidence of the opulence and nobility of their owners in the olden time. There is something very Italian about Ventimiglia. The stalls of maccaroni and polenta are placed, as at Naples, under dark archways, and picturesque young women and grotesque old ones outbawl each other in praise of their goods.

In a general way, M. de Monleon was our *cicerone*, and, well acquainted with the ancient and modern history of the country, added to the interest of every castle, tower, shrine, convent, and river by some romantic story or spirit-stirring legend. But on this occasion M. de Monleon,—who was the spirit of urbanity, politeness, and self-denial,—gave way when he found in Mr. Fenwick a rival antiquarian, very anxious to show his knowledge, and possessed of a very loud voice and a rather overbearing manner.

Mr. Fenwick had evidently studied the

history of Mentone and all the towns of the
Riviera, probably with a view to showing off.
M. de Moulcon only selected, naturally, as
the scenes we were visiting recalled them to
his well-stored memory, those legends and
anecdotes which he had known from his
boyhood.   In order to establish himself as
the *cicerone* of the party, Mr. Fenwick had
alighted from the carriage as we approached
the cathedral, and, leaning on Jock's shoulder
with one hand, he took Harry Blake's arm
with the other, pointing to the cathedral
(which he certainly could not see), informed
us that St. Barnabas had been its first bishop,
and expatiated on the length and picturesque
appearance of the building, on its grey Lom-
bardo-Gothic porch, its singular apse, and
its tall tower.   He then pointed out the
large palace of the Lascaris, dwelling on the
open loggia and grand staircase as if he at
that moment actually beheld them : which

he certainly could only do with his mind's eye.

It was rather affecting to hear the poor fellow expatiating on the fine contrast presented by the bright colouring of the cathedral and the noble background of snowy mountains, that stood " like the ghost of a giant creature gone by," with the torrent flashing and dashing, sporting and darkling over its stony bed in the middle distance.

" But," said Mr. Fenwick, " I remember, when on former occasions I have visited Ventimiglia, at times when I too was an artist, I discovered that the noblest view of all is to be obtained by descending to the very bed of the torrent. When we return I will show you some of my old sketch-books, which I brought with me to compare the scenes of twenty years ago with those of to-day. I think you will agree (although I made several sketches of Ventimiglia from

from different points of view, and coloured some of them) that the most spirited is that taken from the bed of the torrent. There you see the town rising like so many terraces composed of quaint old houses, churches, convents, and towns, backed by mauve-coloured mountains, wearing snow-white caps ; and a very effective foreground to the picture is formed by the long succession of pointed arches of the old bridge, while, for focal relief, I remember the scarlet petticoats of some washerwomen, and the red caps of some fishermen who were talking to them, came in very effectively. But I have my drawing of the scene in my portmanteau, and will show it to you this evening, if you remind me of it."

Mr. Fenwick was about to proceed with his showman-like catalogue of the objects of interest around us, but Lady Beatrice, who had listened with great impatience to the

somewhat pompous and prosy Fenwick, although she never wearied of M. de Moulcon
as a *cicerone*, stepped off her donkey, and
said, " Well, I'm off to San Michele. Lucia
told me exactly how to get to it. Any one
who likes may follow me, and no one need
try to dissuade me, for I'm quite resolved to
lionize that church on the hill."

As she spoke, she laughed and tripped
lightly away, taking a path which turns
aside to the left of the bridge.

M. de Moulcon approached my mother.

" Dear lady," he said, " do not let her go.
It is very unsafe even for a strong man, sure
of foot and not likely to turn giddy; but
for Lady Beatrice, so delicate, so short-
breathed, and so impressionable—let me
say you forbid the rash expedition."

He spoke in Italian very vehemently; his
cheeks were pale with emotion, and his dark
eyes flashed.

"Tell her I implore her not to venture it, but to return at once," said my mother; then added, as M. de Monleon dashed after the wilful girl, "I fear no wish of mine will prevent that wilful girl from doing anything that is likely to tease and terrify M. de Monleon."

My mother was right. Lady Beatrice had passed through the postern-gate, and was panting as she ascended the narrow staircase inside the city walls.

Vainly M. de Monleon called to her, and implored her, in my mother's name, to return. She pretended not to hear him. He therefore resolved to follow her, and share the peril her obstinacy prevented his averting. My mother became very uneasy, but Mr. Fenwick, not at all pleased at being interrupted in his harangue, told her, with an authoritative wave of the hand, that the danger was very much exaggerated; that in former times he had frequently taken the same way to San Michele; and added, that if a man of six feet four neither slipped on the narrow stairs nor toppled over the unprotected overhanging parapets, a sylph-like girl and an under-sized man like M. de Monleon ran very little risk, if any. M. de Monleon was five feet eleven, and most people would have considered him a tall man; but Mr. Fenwick was his own standard of perfection in everything, and he, being six feet four, looked down from his superior altitude on the elegant Alphonse.

Mr. Fenwick was very impatient when he marked the tone of anxiety in my mother's voice, for he was jealous of the entire attention of his hearers, my mother's especially; so raising his voice, knitting his brows, and addressing himself pointedly to her, he said —"The church of San Michele, Mrs. Moore, which edifice I have no doubt your young

friend has safely reached by this time, was originally a temple dedicated to Castor and Pol-
lux; afterwards it became a Benedictine convent. I hope you are following me, madam," he
said to my mother, whose eyes would wander
to the path near the bridge, by which Lady
Beatrice had reached the low postern gate
that led to the staircase in the town wall.

"I am attending, Mr. Fenwick," said my
mother apologetically; " but I cannot help
feeling nervous till I see Lady Beatrice safe
back."

"Then, perhaps," he replied in an offended
tone, " it will not interest you to hear that
there are two Roman mile-stones preserved
near the church—stones of the time of Au-
gustus and Antoninus Pius. But I perceive
I might as well address myself to those very
stones," he said angrily.

" Forgive me, dear friend," said my mother; " I am all attention now, for I see that

wilful girl issuing from the postern gate, flushed with triumph at the feat she has achieved."

But Mr. Fenwick would not resume his discourse. He was, by nature, very passionate and sulky. It is a popular fallacy that passionate people are not, in general, sulky. My experience contradicts this assertion, and so, I imagine, does that of most of my readers. How often do we see two people, after a violent quarrel, avoid each other, and sulk for days, and even weeks!

Mr. Fenwick had been very good-humoured since he had been at Mentone; but there, he had had his own way in everything; nothing had occurred to thwart or annoy him. Now his temper was roused and his vanity wounded by my mother's inattention; and, in his large light eyes, almost sightless though they were, and on his massive, Roman-emperor-like, and stony features, I saw the expression that fully accounted for the terror he was said to have inspired in his wife and child.

We lingered for awhile, admiring the beautiful valley beyond the bridge, from which the church tower is seen to great advantage, and M. de Monleon persuaded us to adjourn to Albergo della Scalata, and to order some fruit, bread, and wine, by way of luncheon. Of this refreshment we partook on the flat, balustraded roof of the inn, and enjoyed, from that spot, a delightful and extensive view of the antique town and the noble castle crowning the opposite heights.

I could see that Lady Beatrice and Alphonse de Monleon were not quite as friendly as usual. I thought it very likely, as he was very frank and rather fiery, he might have censured her for her rashness in venturing up the perilous ascent, and perhaps have alluded, reproachfully, to the anxiety she had caused my mother. Beatrice would bear rebuke from my dear gentle mother, and even from myself; but I felt certain she would not tamely submit to it from Alphonse de Monleon. Her eyes looked unnaturally bright, and she had a brilliant colour; I had never seen her look so beautiful. But her lovely lips had a scornful expression; and when Alphonse, who watched her lovely face with his soul in his eyes, offered her anything, or spoke to her, she answered him coldly, and by monosyllables only.

With two of the party out of humour, the luncheon, in spite of the good wine, fine fruit, and a nice sort of cake, and in spite, too, of the glorious sun lighting up all the beauties of that happy valley, was rather silent and constrained. However, before we left the flat roof of the inn, Mr. Fenwick had recovered himself sufficiently to remark

to M. de Monleon that Ventimiglia, in
ancient times, was called Albium Inteme-
lium, and was the capital of a Ligurian race
called the Intemelians. He added, that
peaceful as the scene was now, it had been
one of constant warfare in the middle ages;
and that while the Lascaris family held the
fortress, it was constantly the object of
assault; the Dukes of Savoy, the Counts of
Parma, and the Genoese, all trying, in turn,
to obtain possession of a stronghold which
formed a sort of entrance to the kingdom of
Piedmont. My mother, whose very kind
heart had reproached her with the offence
she had given, drew near to Mr. Fenwick
as he spoke, and listened with so much attention, that he gradually recovered his good
humour, and proposed that we should proceed to Bordighera.

CHAPTER XXII.

BORDIGHERA.

January 15*th*.—-Bordighera is enchanted ground, but that enchantment, lovely as the spot really is, may be traced rather to the wand of genius than to that of nature.

Bordighera did not rank as a place of great importance to the artist or the tourist until Signor Ruffini made it the scene of a tale which, strictly speaking, neither novel nor romance, has yet the best charms of both, and in its sublime simplicity of plot and construction, with its fresh nature and purity of style, reminds one at once of two very different *chefs-d'œuvre*—'Paul and Virginia' and the 'Vicar of Wakefield.'

It is amazing what the genius of the poet and the novelist can do to make of "airy nothings a local habitation and a name."

What pilgrimages have been made by admirers of the Prospero of the North—the immortal Walter Scott—to every moor or morass, hall or hovel, castle or cot, barn or brae, over which he had shed the sunshine of his genius! And thus, as we drew near Bordighera, we began to look out—not for the castle or the hilly coast, the grim promontory or the distant Antibes — but for the Osteria where that passionate drama of two young hearts opened so sweetly, and for every spot where Antonio and Lucy had been.

To my excited fancy, a young mountaineer talking earnestly to a dark-eyed Speranza were the humble lovers of the story, and Lady Beatrice and M. de Monleon were no bad impersonations of the gentle Lucy and the immortal Antonio.

I tried even to make a Sir John out of the purblind Mr. Fenwick, but it would not do ; the blindness of Sir John was purely figurative, and though he was a very fair representative of a rather kind-hearted, narrow-minded, prejudiced class, Mr. Fenwick, with his learning, his intellect, and his originality of character, was not to be brought down to the level of a man who had no distinction but his title.

The road from Ventimiglia to Bordighera is very flat and dusty. There is nothing of the savage grandeur and sublimity of Ventimiglia or Roccabruna in this tract of country, which is studded with villas, just as Clapham and the Isle of Wight are; but once on the handsome stone bridge that spans the river, there is a glorious view of the snowy mountains up its valley, and of. the noble ruins of the Castle of Dolceaqua.

Mr. Fenwick, addressing himself to my mother, rather pompously informed her that Bordighera had been called " the Jericho of Italy ;" that the town contained no object of interest, but that palm-trees of great beauty and laden with dates and flowers of wondrous hues and fragrance, adorned the gardens of the French Consul.

My mother, however, who had a tinge of poetry and romance in her character, would not agree that there was nothing of interest in Bordighera.

There was still a great deal of youth of heart and freshness of feeling about my mother, and she wanted to fix on the spot where first Lucy essayed to walk after her accident,—to fix on Dr. Antonio's house,— and to make sure which was the Osteria.

All this Mr. Fenwick treated with ill-disguised contempt.

"Who is this Dr. Antonio, of whom you are all so full?" he said.

When told that he was an imaginary character, the hero of a novel, he became very stern and sullen.

"Novels are story-books," he said, "and story-books are fit only for children! I am happy to say I never read a novel in my life—and what is more, I never mean to!"

He grew silent and sulky after this, and, to punish what he considered to be the frivolity of my mother and the rest of the party, he locked up in his own mind a very erudite, wordy, and pedantic history of Bordighera which he got up from his old journal, note-book, and gazetteer, to enlighten us with, as soon as we should have reached the common at the hill-top.

I believe he had enriched this discourse

with short accounts of all the old towns to
be seen from the emerald promontory of
Bordighera. Ventimiglia, Mentone, Roccabruna, Turbia, Villa Franca, and Monaco
were all to have had their story told; so that
in all probability the shades of evening
would have closed around us, and, worse
still, the cold night breeze would have come
forth to chill the delicate Lady Beatrice,
but for Mr. Fenwick's sudden and fortunate
fit of ill-temper.

When once he began a discourse, no one
could stop him; but, luckily, he was so very
touchy, jealous, and vindictive, that he took
offence very easily, and then he became
sullenly silent, often for hours together.

Harry Blake and M. de Monleon did their
best to atone to the ladies of the party for
Mr. Fenwick's rudeness. They gathered
beautiful ferns, mosses, and wild flowers,
and brought them to us; and we took out

our sketch-books to take views of Dolce-aqua's noble ruins.

But the evident tiff or coldness between Alphonse de Monleon and Lady Beatrice threw a sort of restraint over the party, independently of the increasing scowls of Mr. Fenwick.

"Oh, good temper! angel of life," said Harry Blake aside to me, as he noticed the frown on Lady Beatrice's fair brow, the angry glance of her eyes, and the curl of her lip. "Oh, good temper, thou art as essential to the enjoyment of a picnic abroad, and to a fireside at home, as is the sun to a landscape or a smile to the face of beauty. I could dispense," he added warmly, "with personal charms, genius, accomplishments, grace, charms; but that which irradiates the plainest face, gives softness to the voice, enchantment to the intercourse, peace to the dwelling, and security to the wedded state

—good temper, that I could not dispense with; and as that is the rarest of gifts I shall probably die a bachelor.

"Sweet, lovely, and elegant as Lady Beatrice is, she is not

> "'Blest with temper whose unclouded ray
>   Can make to-morrow cheerful as to-day;
>   She who ne'er answers till a husband cools,
>   And tho' she rules him never shows she rules,
>   Charms by accepting, by submitting sways,
>   And has her humour most when she obeys.'

However, I only hold with Pope's *beau idéal* of a wife as far as the good temper goes; the latter part of the quotation conveys to my mind the idea of a cunning, manœuvring woman,—a sort of woman only one degree less odious than a shrill-tongued, jealous shrew."

As the wind was rising and shaking the unripe dates from the palm-trees, and my mother began to fear it might soon be too chilly for the delicate Beatrice, and as two

of the party were so cross and so disagreeable
I proposed that we should sit at home.

Lady Beatrice had coughed several times,
and, at my mother's entreaty, had taken out
her handkerchief, which was beautifully
worked and trimmed with lace, to tie round
her throat. She was in the act of adjusting
it, when, by some accident, it dropped from
her hand, and before she could recover it—
before indeed any one could pick it up, the
wind carried it away, and, wafting it across
a fissure in the rocks, bore it on, on, on,
until it was caught by a branch of a tree
that rose from a craggy projection of a precipitous rock.

"Oh, my handkerchief!" cried Lady
Beatrice, bursting into tears. "What shall
I do? It was my dear, dear mother's, and
was marked with her hair. I would rather
have lost everything I have in the world
than that dear relic."

Those words, and the sobs that accompanied, reached the ears of Alphonse de Monleon. Truly passion is a sort of madness. Who loves, raves, says Byron; and lovers often act as raving lunatics would do if they were free. He darted from the tree against which he was leaning—pale, absorbed, with knitted brows and folded arms. He cleared the fissure in the rock at a bound.

"Good heavens!" cried Harry Blake, "he is not going to risk his life for a bit of muslin. That is a tufa rock, and is sure to give way with him."

He shouted to him to stop, but Monleon heeded him not.

Lady Beatrice uttered a piercing shriek; the rest of the party looked on, hushed and livid with horror and alarm.

In safety Alphonse de Monleon climbed that steep and perilous ascent. He reached the tree, took the handkerchief from the

branch that had caught it, waved it in the
air, folded it, and put it in his bosom, and
was about to retrace his steps when the
crumbling tufa rock gave way. A landslip
had taken place, as Mr. Fenwick had pro-
phesied it would, and down, down, down
went Alphonse de Monleon, till he reached
the valley below, where he lay apparently
lifeless.

"This way! this way!" cried one of the
donkey-drivers; "this is the best way to the
valley." Pale with horror, we followed the
lad.

It seemed a long time before we reached
the spot; when we did so, we saw Alphonse
lying in a sort of huddled mass. His up-
turned face was as the face of the dead; his
black hair was dabbled with blood, and lay
in a pool of gore.

I did not know that Lady Beatrice had
followed us to the valley until a piercing

shriek rent the air, a woman's shriek—a
cry of despair from the heart of a loving
woman—and then Beatrice darted forward,
and, unmindful of everything but Alphonse
and the passion she had so long and so well
concealed, she threw herself on her knees
beside him, and cried as she tossed her arms
wildly up, " Oh, Alphonse ! oh, my beloved !
oh, speak to me ! look at me, smile on me.
No ! no ! no ! you cannot be dead, I will not
believe it ; but if you are, I will not survive
you, my love, my life, my Alphonse !"

Strange to say, at that moment, every one
present was so absorbed by horror, that Lady
Beatrice's passionate confession excited very
little notice.   Harry Blake was the first to
recover some degree of presence of mind.
He asked my mother if she had any smelling
salts, eau de Cologne, or any other restorative
with her.   Fortunately she had both.

He approached Alphonse de Monleon and

knelt by his side. He was about to bathe
his brow and moisten his lips and nostrils
with the eau de Cologne, when Lady Beatrice snatched them from him, exclaiming,
" Give the bottle to me, I will bathe his dear
brow; and the salts, let me have them. Do
you see if you can stanch the blood still
flowing from that wound in his beautiful,
beloved head."

What a subject for Millais would have
been that scene!--Alphonse de Monleon, his
fine Italian face pale as that of the dead,
his eyelids closed, and the long black lashes
resting on the livid cheeks; his fine form
lying on the blood-stained sod of the valley,
and that fragile, lovely girl, bending over
him, her white shawl and fair hands stained
with his blood, her large blue eyes fixed
on his face; soul, heart, and mind, all bleed
in that earnest gaze.

Harry Blake was supporting his head, and

the rest of the party, pale and trembling, looking on in dismay.

Luckily, my mother's smelling-salts were very strong, and as Beatrice held them to Alphonse de Monleon's nostrils, a faint tinge of colour stole over his death-like cheek. A sort of sob, or something between a sob and a sigh, convulsed his breast; he opened his eyes, and beholding Beatrice bending over him, a smile of love ineffable played on his white lips.

"Alphonse! dear Alphonse!" cried Beatrice, wild with joy and hope. "Oh, Heaven be praised, you are not dead! Live, live, Alphonse! you know how I love you!"

Beatrice spoke in Italian, of which language she was perfect mistress: the aunt, who had taken charge of her when her mother died, was an Italian.

Alphonse's whole countenance became flushed and irradiated with joy and love as he heard these words :—"Tu m'ami," he cried, "tu m'ami. O Dio, O Beatrice mia, moro còntento."

He raised himself a little, with a wild effort clasped her bending form to his breast, and sank back again insensible.

"We must remove him to the nearest house," said Harry Blake, "and a surgeon must be procured immediately."

"Lady Beatrice," he said, "let me entreat you to give way; his life depends on his being removed to the nearest house, and attended by a surgeon."

But Beatrice made no reply, and when Harry would gently have assisted her to rise, he found that she had fainted. Harry Blake lifted her light form from Alphonse's embrace, and placed her on the grass, where my mother and I had spread a warm thick shawl to receive her.

We succeeded in restoring her to consciousness, and by that time Harry, Jock, and two donkey-drivers were carrying Alphonse de Monleon in a plaid Mr. Fenwick had brought with him, to the nearest abode.

It was not the Osteria, but it was a tolerably comfortable cottage, and the hospitable mistress, a widow, placed everything in her house at our disposal.

Alphonse was placed on a bed, and the nearest doctor was sent for. He was not a Dr. Antonio, but he was an intelligent, experienced, elderly man. He said everything would depend on entire repose—on the total exclusion of all light, all noise. It was a case of concussion of the brain, but the' blood which had flowed so freely from the wound had probably prevented its being suddenly fatal, and, on the whole, he had more hope than fear.

He wished that Dr. B—— and a celebrated Italian physician, very popular at

Mentone, should be sent for, as he wished to have a consultation with them. He also desired that a nurse should be provided; and then he strongly advised, as M. de Monleon at the very best could not possibly be moved for some days, that Harry Blake and Jock should remain in attendance on M. de Monleon, and that the rest of the party should return to Mentone.

I never saw an expression of such anguish on a human face as I perceived on that of Beatrice as she heard the doctor urge our departure.

The doctor left us, to steal on tiptoe to his patient's bedside; and then Beatrice, the proud, aristocratic, high-spirited Beatrice, drew near my mother, and sinking on her knees before her, said, "Oh, Mrs. Moore, for pity's sake, for Heaven's sake, for my sake, do not let us go and leave *him* here, perhaps to die! I cannot go. I am certain

I should not live through the night—the night that may be his last. Say you will stay," she cried, seizing my mother's hand and covering it with her kisses and her tears. " We have plenty of warm cloaks and shawls; let us pass the night here. Let Mr. Fenwick and Jock go back to Mentone, and send dear old Bessie to help us to nurse him. Send Dr. B—— and Dr. —— to consult with the surgeon; but unless you would see me die, do not refuse to stay."

My mother, who was extremely anxious about the interesting young man of whom we had seen so much, and who had endeared himself to us all by his noble nature, sweet temper, and elegant manners, raised Lady Beatrice, and, tenderly embracing her, promised all she required.

Mr. Fenwick, in his very worst humour, for no one had taken any notice of him since the accident—Jock always excepted—left

Bordighera in the carriage, accompanied by his " eye."

Alphonse's room had been completely darkened. He was in bed, apparently asleep.

The doctor, whose name was Carrara, took his seat by his side to listen to his breathing. The bedroom door was closed, and Harry Blake, Lady Beatrice, and I wrapped ourselves up in the cloaks and shawls we had brought with us, and prepared to get through the night as well as we could, comforting ourselves with the reflection that Bessie, provided with every kind of comfort and restorative and herself the best of nurses, would be with us at dawn, probably accompanied by Dr. B—— and Signor ——.

My mother and myself were so worn out with the excitement and fatigue of this eventful day, that we slept, although we were supplied with nothing better than two wooden stools. But whenever I woke—and

I did so several times—I could see by the glorious light of the moonlight, the anxious, restless Lady Beatrice either kneeling in fervent prayer, or standing at Alphonse's door listening intently, or pacing restlessly up and down the little outer chamber in which we were.

CHAPTER XXIII.

ARRIVAL OF HELP.

January 16*th*.—Day was just beginning to dawn, when her quick ear distinguished the sound of wheels.

"They come! they come!" she cried. "Oh, Heaven be praised! Dr. B—— is come. If any one can save Alphonse, he can."

Beatrice was right. Dr. B——, Signor ——, and honest Bessie, with abundance of sheets, pillows, restoratives, and comforts of all kinds, had arrived.

Signor Carrara had heard the carriage, and, nevertheless, left his patient and joined us in the outer room. After some conversation between the three medical men, they adjourned to the patient's apartment. After about an hour spent in whispered consultation, as far as possible from Alphonse's bed, Dr. B—— came into our room and summoned Bessie.

"Dr. B—— !" cried Lady Beatrice, clasping his arm; "can you save him? Will he live?"

"I hope so, my dear lady—my poor child," said Dr. B—— almost tenderly. "I think we shall save him."

Lady Beatrice seized the Doctor's hand and pressed it to her lips.

CHAPTER XXIV.

OUT OF DANGER.

January 16th.—We passed about two hours in the greatest anxiety and suspense. Lady Beatrice, at times, was almost frantic—wringing her hands, beating her breast, and tearing her hair. Then she would fling herself on her knees and pray fervently, then throw herself into my arms or my mother's, and weep on our bosoms. Several times Bessie came in to fetch water-basins, towels, and brandy. She looked pale and anxious,—she seemed in a great hurry, and we did not delay her by asking any questions. We were, in fact, afraid to question her ; we dreaded her answers.

*　　*　　*　　*　　*

Another hour, during which we had been electrified by a sharp cry of pain, and several groans, and then Dr. B—— came in and said—

"All danger is over, my dear ladies. With patience and quiet Monsieur de Monleon will now do very well. Signor Carrara, Bessie, and Mr. Blake will remain with him ; and I must now, as your family physician, order you all back to Mentone,—my fair patient, Lady Beatrice, especially, who looks as if this night's watch had been rather too much for her."

"You are sure he is out of danger, Doctor ? " said Lady Beatrice.

"Quite sure. I wish I were as certain that you are, my dear young friend," said

Dr. B—— resolutely, drawing her arm within his, and leading her to his brougham, in which he conveyed her, my mother, and myself back to Mentone.

CHAPTER XXV.

ALPHONSE'S RECOVERY.

February 30*th.*—It was a fortnight before M. de Monleon was able to quit the cottage at Bordighera. All the time he was there Lady Beatrice was in a fever of anxiety, and could not rest unless my mother and I would go directly after breakfast with her to Maritana's cot; nor could she bear to go back to Mentone till night-fall, when Dr. B—— took us back in his brougham.

Dr. B—— told my mother that a part of M. de Monleon's skull, coming in contact where he fell with a sharp point of rock, a slight fracture or dint had ensued, and that it had been found necessary, in order to save his reason, and perhaps his life, to trepan him. He had borne the operation with the greatest fortitude, and the result had been most satisfactory.

During the greater part of this time Mr. Fenwick had kept aloof. He could not bear to find us all engrossed by anxiety about Alphonse de Monleon, to the exclusion of all interest in himself. He remained a good deal at the Hôtel des Quatre Nations with Harry Bláke and Jock. The former he kept constantly engaged in reading to him the old histories of the principalities of Mentone and its neighbouring towns, or in writing a *précis* of the same from his dictation.

No doubt Mr. Fenwick meant to astonish us all with his erudition and knowledge of the ancient history of the Riviera, as soon as we should be able to resume our excursions.

It was a real *fête* for us all, when Alphonse de Monleon was allowed to return to Mentone and to resume his ordinary habits and mode of life.

Although we three ladies, my mother, Lady Beatrice, and myself, had been daily to Bordighera, we had none of us seen Alphonse de Monleon since his accident. The doctors, both English and Italian, agreed in forbiding anything that could tend to excite him. He was not even permitted to know that we were at Maritana's cottage; but he probably guessed it, as he seemed perfectly happy and resigned.

Lady Beatrice and Alphonse de Monleon had not met since, in the agony and terror of her heart, she had so suddenly revealed to every one present that passion which she had till then so wondrously concealed, that no one, not even I, who was very intimate with her, or at least fancied I was so, had the slightest notion of it.

Poor Beatrice! not only had she betrayed her secret to the whole party, but to Alphonse himself.

As the time for his arrival at our house drew near, the dear girl was in an agitation piteous and painful to behold; now trembling like an aspen-leaf and deadly pale, her bosom panting, her hands tightly clasped, and tears in her eyes; anon flushed, haughty, erect, and apparently resolved to ignore all that passed, all that had escaped her in the agony of her terror, and to return to her assumed coldness and disdain.

I was in my dear mother's room a little while before Alphonse de Monleon and Dr. B—— were expected to come to dine with us, and I perceived in my mother's pale face an expression of perplexity and distress not habitual with her : deep sorrow had been ever since my father's death the characteristic of those beautiful features.

"Ada," she said, "I am uneasy in my mind about Lady Beatrice."

"How so, dear mother?" I replied. "She seems to me to be much improved in health since she has been here."

"I do not speak of her health, dearest," said my mother, "but of this passionate attachment which she has conceived for M. de Monleon, and which she had so well concealed that I really believed, till she betrayed herself in her terror and distress, that she disliked him. Had I imagined it possible she would have fallen in love with him, I should have discouraged all intimacy; much as I like him myself, I should never have invited him to come here or to join us in our excursions."

"But why not, Mamma? Alphonse de

Monleon is a man of very noble and ancient family; good, honourable, amiable, accomplished. Why should he not be Lady Beatrice's accepted suitor?"

"Because her father, Lord Lorraine, is one of the proudest of our English peers, and he would never consent to the marriage of his only child with M. de Monleon, who, however ancient his birth and admirable in himself, is the descendant of a ruined though noble family, and has scarcely three hundred a year to live on, and that sum derived from letting the Maison de Monleon to English visitors."

"Poor Beatrice! what will become of her," I cried, "and Alphonse de Monleon, who idolizes her? To lose her will be a deathblow to him."

"At any rate," said my mother, "now that he knows that Lady Beatrice loves him —it has been long clear to every one that he

adores her—there is but one course open to
him as a man of honour. He must write to
her father and beg his permission to pay his
addresses to Lady Beatrice. I have no
doubt he will see the necessity of at once
taking this step. Should he not, it will be
my duty to suggest it; but I own to you,
my dear Ada, that I fear the result will be
the removal of Lady Beatrice from this
place, and her father's scornful rejection of
poor Alphonse's offer, and prohibition of all
future intercourse."

" Alas!" I cried, "what a cruel father he
must be if he acts thus! Lady Beatrice is
very delicate ; but since she has been here,
and has felt happy in the love she has inspired and reciprocated, she has been a new
creature. I am certain if Lord Lorraine
tears her away from Alphonse de Monleon,
she will not live long."

" Another great objection," said' my mother, "would be M. de Monleon's religion. He is a Roman Catholic."

"I don't think that would matter," I replied; "for Beatrice tells me her own mother was a Roman Catholic; and but for the aunt, to whom she was confided when she was a child after her mother's death, she too would have been a Romanist. At any rate, dear mother," I added, "say nothing to Alphonse or to Beatrice to-day. Let this, the first day of his return amongst us, be a festival. To-morrow, if he says nothing on the subject, you can tell him all you think on the subject; but let the poor fellow be happy to-day."

My mother agreed to this, and I went to my own room to dress for dinner.

Lucia, who was in attendance on me, told me with arch smiles and many blushes that Lady Beatrice had been ready more than an hour, and was in the drawing-room when

Dr. B—— arrived with M. de Monleon,—
that the doctor had a patient to visit before
coming to dinner, and that he had left M.
de Monleon and Lady Beatrice together.

" How they love each other !" said Lucia ;
" how happy they will be !"

I only answered with a sigh. Alas ! after
what my mother had said, I was tempted to
exclaim, " How miserable they will be !"

I loitered over my toilet as long as I could,
hating to rob these devoted lovers of the
few happy moments fate had allowed them ;
but at last I heard Dr. B——'s carriage stop
at the gate, and my dear mother ring her
bell for Bessie. I hurried downstairs, that
Alphonse and Lady Beatrice might not be
found *tête-à-tête.* I knew how proud and
shy the dear girl was.

As I opened the door, Alphonse rose from
his knees before Lady Beatrice, and she,
covered with blushes, dashed away the tears

from her cheeks and hastened to the window. There were tears in Alphonse's dark eyes too, but an expression of ineffable happiness was on his fine face. I saw the same radiant and almost celestial joy in Beatrice's violet eyes and lovely countenance when she took her place at the dinner table.

M. de Monleon was in high spirits. Mr. Fenwick was of the party, so full of the lore he had been acquiring during the last fortnight that it burst out almost in spite of himself; and before the soup was removed he had contrived to introduce the Roman dominion, the Saracen invasion, Giballino Grimaldi, the Genoese, the Guelphs and Ghibellines, and Charles Grimaldi. My mother, who was very anxious to keep Mr. Fenwick in good humour,—she was attached to him because he was so devoted to my father,—listened so attentively to his rather pedantic harangue, that he promised in the

course of the evening to give her a sketch
of the early history of Monaco and Mentone,
and the names of all their early rulers.

"The history of Mentone," said Mr. Fenwick, taking out a note-book, which, however, he could not decipher, "is so mixed
up with that of Monaco that they are one
and the same, and both are but the narrative
of the fortunes and misfortunes of the Grimaldi family, who have governed Monaco
ever since the State sprang into existence.
It was not till the end of the twelfth century
that Monaco became of any importance; till
then it was merely a barren rock, and a re-
fuge, or rather a port in a storm, for ships
coasting Liguria and Provence. According
to Dionysius of Halicarnassus," continued
Mr. Fenwick pompously, "Hercules here
built a temple to himself: this temple was
the abode of one hermit or monk—hence
the name 'Monaco.' Some historians say

the place owes its name and origin to the
Phocæans. Long before the city was built,
the Portus Herculis was known and valued."

Here Colonel Ridley and Violet, who were
with us upon this occasion, rose to depart.
We had not seen much of them for some time
past; and my mother, seeing Mr. Fenwick's
checks flush and his eyes flash fire, begged
them to remain to hear the rest of Mr. Fenwick's interesting lecture.

Mr. Fenwick, however, seemed too much
offended to continue his discourse, and, asking Harry for his arm, he went out on the
balcony.

END OF VOL. II.

PRINTED BY J. E. TAYLOR AND CO.,
LITTLE QUEEN STREET, LINCOLN'S INN FIELDS.